THE AUTOMATIC AGE

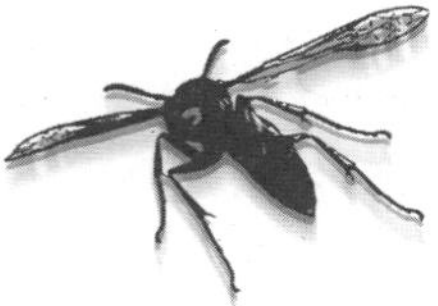

Written and Illustrated by
GMB CHOMICHUK

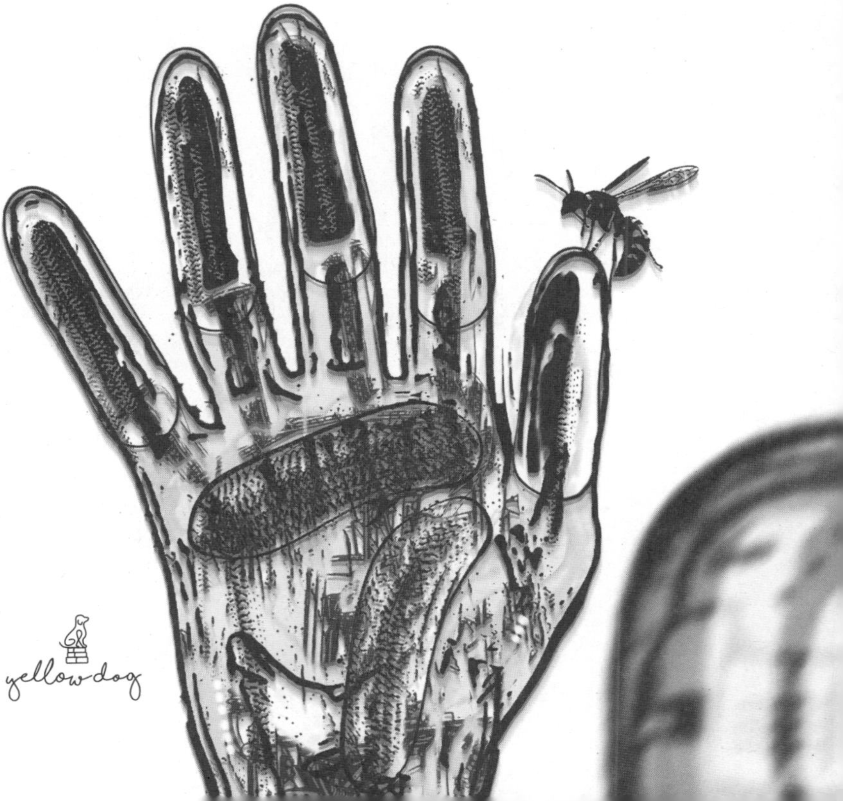

yellow dog

Copyright © 2020 GMB Chomichuk
Yellow Dog
(an imprint of Great Plains Publications)
1173 Wolseley Avenue
Winnipeg, MB R3G 1H1
www.greatplains.mb.ca

Great Plains Publications gratefully acknowledges the financial support
provided for its publishing program by the Government of Canada through
the Canada Book Fund; the Canada Council for the Arts; the Province of
Manitoba through the Book Publishing Tax Credit and the Book Publisher
Marketing Assistance Program; and the Manitoba Arts Council.

Front cover by GMB Chomichuk
Design assistance by Relish New Brand Experience
Printed in Canada by Friesens

LIBRARY AND ARCHIVES CANADA CATALOGUING IN PUBLICATION

Title: Automatic age / Gregory Chomichuk.
Names: Chomichuk, G. M. B., author, illustrator.
Identifiers: Canadiana (print) 20200188917 | Canadiana (ebook)
    20200188968 | ISBN 9781773370408 (softcover) | ISBN 9781773370415
    (ebook)
Classification: LCC PN6733.C536 A98 2020 | DDC 741.5/971—dc23

ENVIRONMENTAL BENEFITS STATEMENT

Great Plains Publications saved the following
resources by printing the pages of this book on
chlorine free paper made with 100% post-consumer
waste.

TREES	WATER	ENERGY	SOLID WASTE	GREENHOUSE GASES
6	480	3	21	2,610
FULLY GROWN	GALLONS	MILLION BTUs	POUNDS	POUNDS

Environmental impact estimates were made using the Environmental Paper Network
Paper Calculator 4.0. For more information visit www.papercalculator.org.

Canadä

FSC
www.fsc.org
MIX
Paper from
responsible sources
FSC® C016245

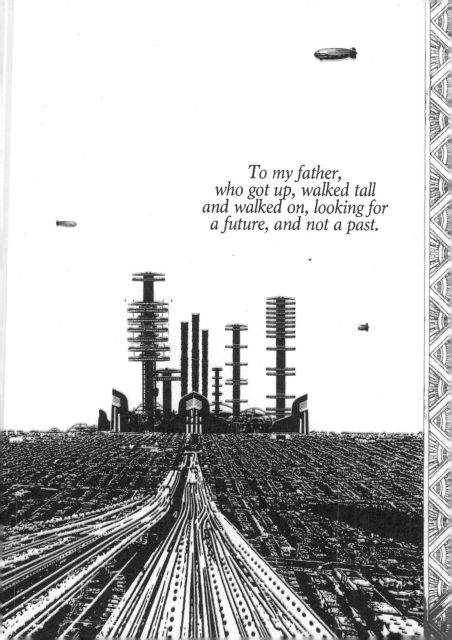

To my father,
who got up, walked tall
and walked on, looking for
a future, and not a past.

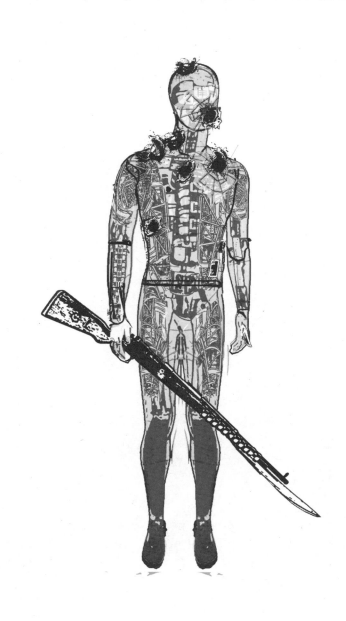

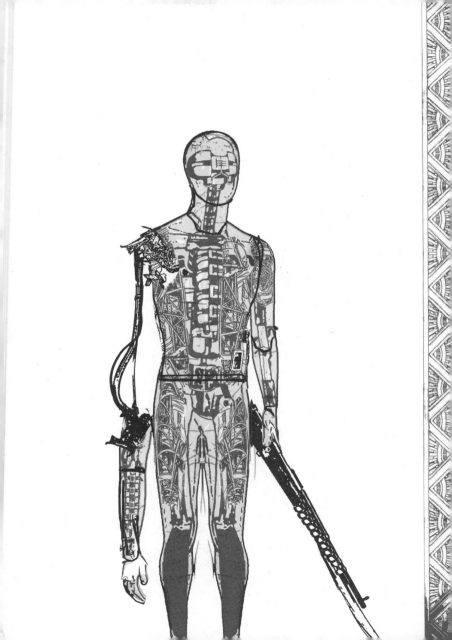

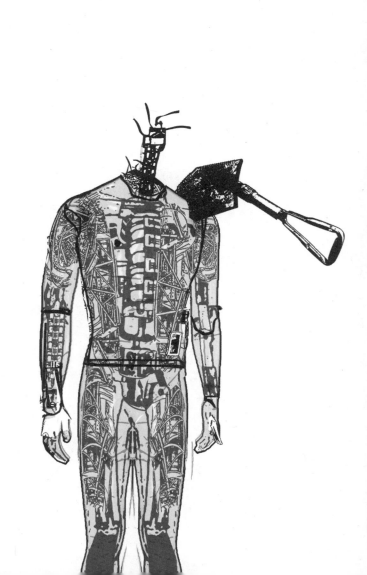

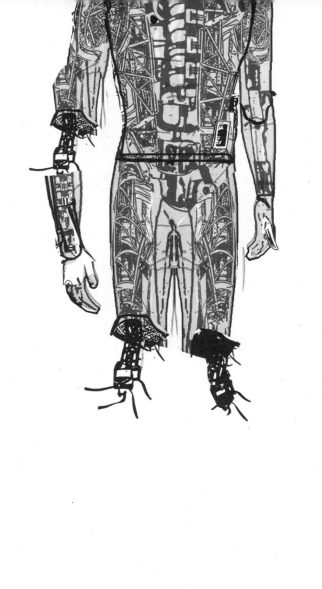

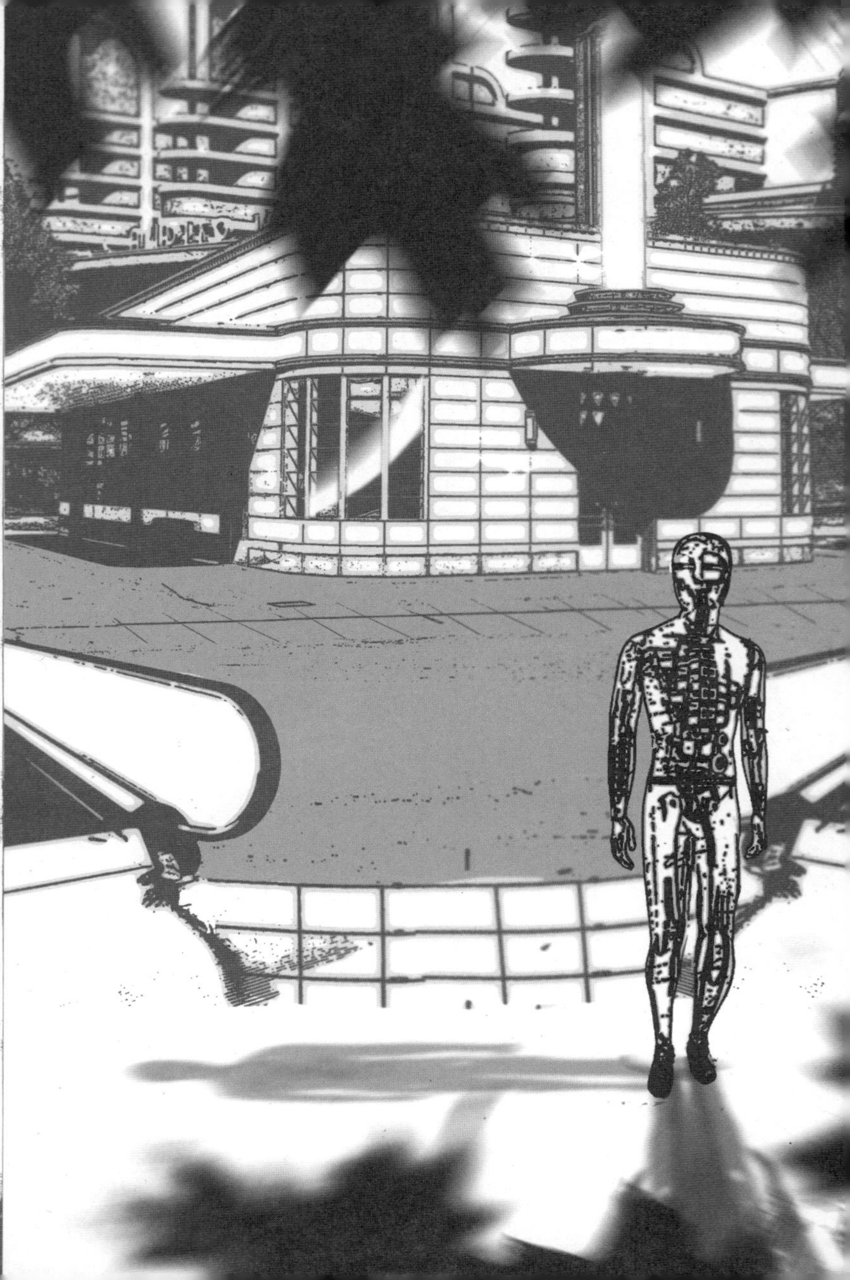

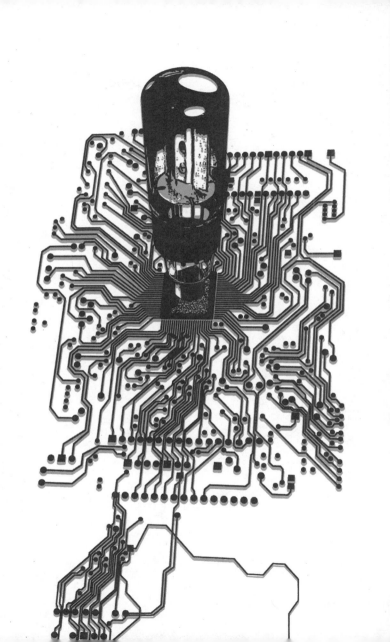

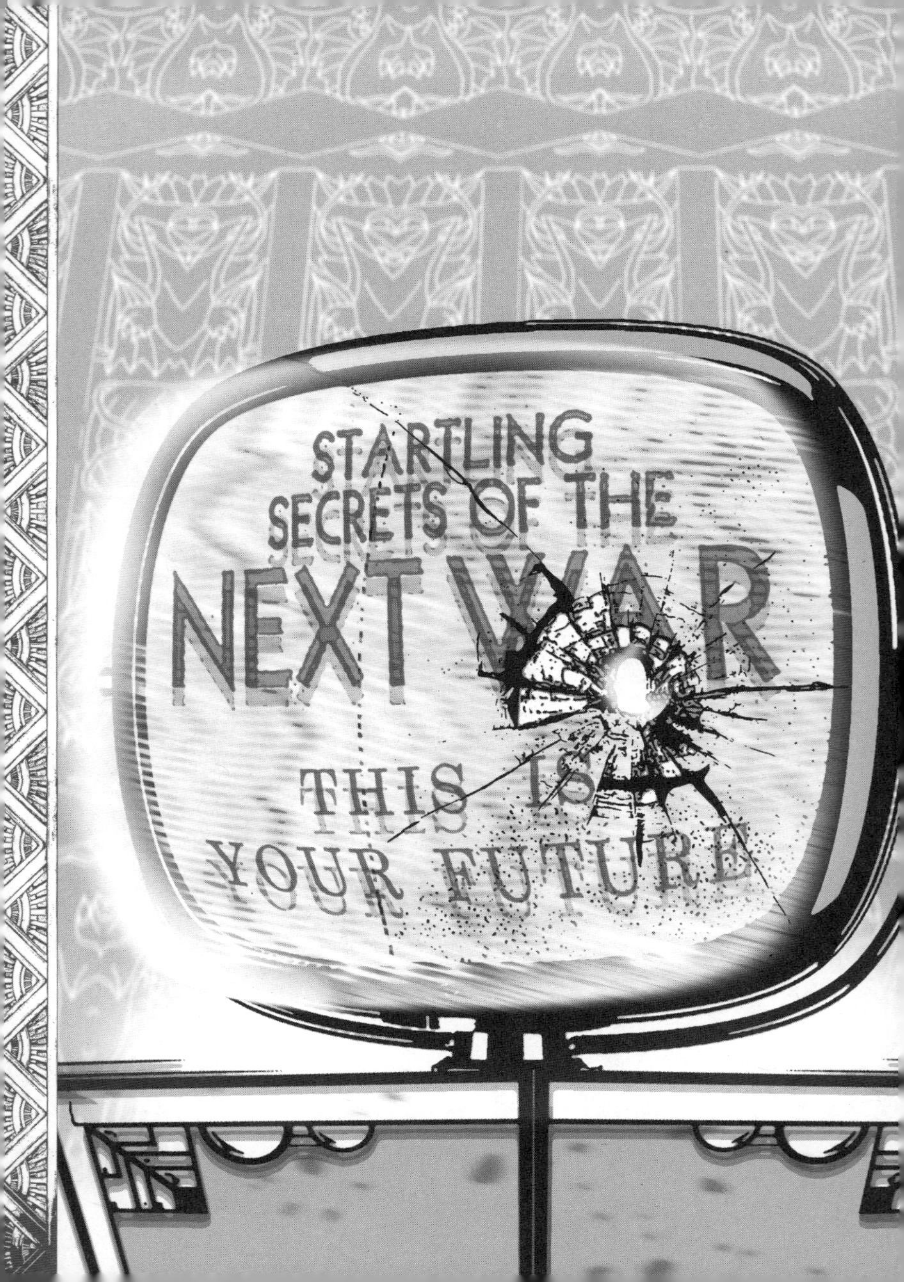
STARTLING
SECRETS OF THE
NEXT WAR
THIS IS
YOUR FUTURE

//THE AUTOMATIC AGE//

//DAYDREAMER//

Kerion had taken the marker tablet three minutes ago, as prescribed. He thumbed the DayDreamer control. He was careful not to dislodge the diode from his forehead. The switch snapped over, and then he was sitting with his brother in the warm glow of the past. The marker was off again. Not quite in the right place. The memory was sooner than it should have been. The machine had again not lived up to its advertised promise of reliving the memory he marked. It was close, and the memory at full magnified recall was intense even in its banality:

"Do you think, thirty years ago, people took it for granted as much as they do now?" Kerion said, just as he had.

"What?" Mark was asking, just as he had.

"Do you think people looked at our present, their future, and thought: There, right there and then, it will be better."

"That's what we do now."

"That's what I'm saying. Aren't you listening?"

"I'm just looking at this. Have you seen this? Remember when robots were toys? They're making robots that fight like men. Like people. They even sort of look like people."

"I'm saying that we are future-obsessed. No one ever looks around and says, 'Ah The Present. Just as I hoped it would be.' You know?"

"Why make them like us? Like people. You can make 'em like anything. Anything. Give 'em treads and a dozen arms. I expect those makers to use their imaginations."

"What?"

"Now you're not listening. The robots. In the war. They make them like people. Arms, legs, head, torso. But why? Why not make them more elaborate. Improve on a human soldier. Oh, shoot man, I'm sorry, you know I— I didn't mean—"

"It's fine. You forgot. That's a good thing. But it's obvious why they make 'em like us."

"Okay, but why?"

"Because to win a war in a way worth winning, you need to get rid of the people but not the structures. The most efficient shape for door-to-door fighting is human.

It's a human world. Doorknobs, ladders, stairs. Buttons, keyboards, cars. To get everyone without damage to the structures, you need to navigate the same environment the same way. Heck, I bet they are making them think like us."

"Oh, you mean obsessed with the future."

"You were listening."

"Of course. Come on. We're late."

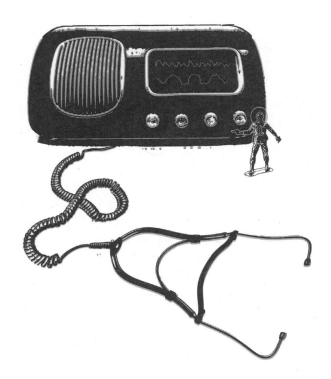

//WORTHTHEWATTS//

"What are you doing, Dad?" Barry said

"What. Oh, sorry I was just—"

"Oh. You were using it again. Couldn't tell with the lights off."

"I was."

"You told me the DayDreamer wasn't worth the watts."

"Did I say that?"

"Why can't *I* try it?"

"The damn thing can only show us the past." Kerion said, then held up the manual and squinted through the dim light. "It says it, '*reads the pleasant topics on our minds and goes back to past moments, with the help of the patented Pleasant Pill*'. You take a pill and remember, then when you '*take the pill again and connect to the DayDreamer it does the remembering for you*'."

"But if you can remember already why do you need it?"

"Well, it's supposed to give you all the details you can't remember normally."

Barry was quiet.

"I guess the assumption was that nostalgia would make you feel better."

"What's nostalgia?"

"A drug," Kerion said dully.

"A drug?"

"No. Not really. Nostalgia is the way to remember things and be happy. But sometimes, all those happy memories make you sad."

"That's because you're an adult."

"What?"

"Adults have lots of junk in there. Don't you remember? You said that to Mom when she got it."

"Oh, yeah. I remember."

"Well. I'm a *kid*. Up until last Christmas, I played and went to school and had vid time. If *I* use it, I bet I'll like it."

"I bet you would. All right."

"Really?"

"Sure."

"What was your DayDream?"

"It was…it was about Uncle Mark. A conversation we had before…. Before."

"Before last Christmas."

"Right."

"I hope I can DayDream Uncle Mark. I miss him."

"Then I hope you do too."

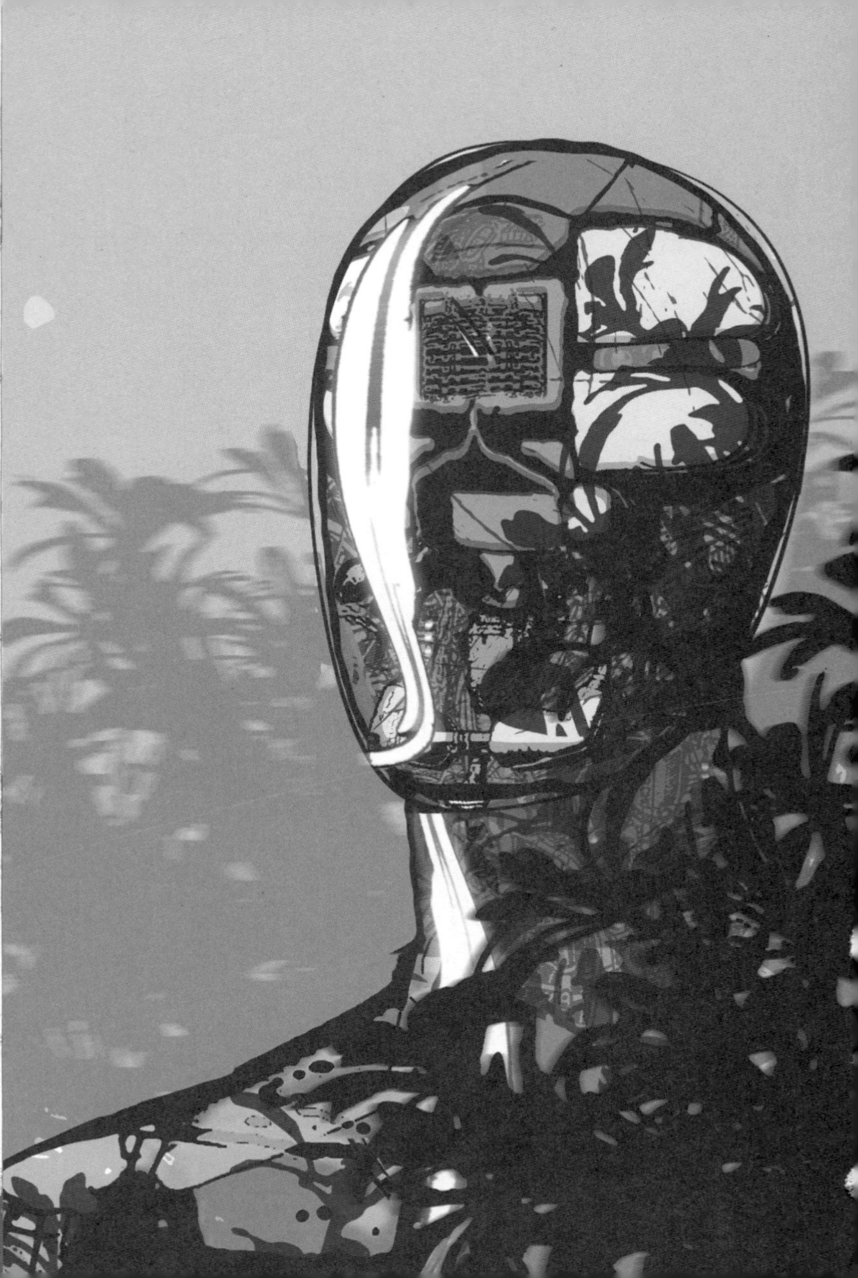

//JOGGER//

The highway racks hummed at night. The grooves set into the slipcrete blinked on as they always did after sunset. The carpods shot past at speed in the three dozen lanes that marked the edge of their forage territory. Kerion wondered about the drivers, locked inside on their endless circuit. Unable to sabotage their perfectly safe carriages. Unable to open them at speed. Some had starved, he thought. Some must have found a way—asphyxiation with the seatbelt. Maybe something sharp in a purse. A pocket knife, maybe.

The freeway lifted in a dozen directions in the centre lanes near Brixton, where they left its well-lit curbs and made their way into automat districts.

They had brought coins aplenty. At first, they had brought the food home, all they could carry, but it spoiled too soon. They had to keep the power low or the auto-volts would come. That meant no refrigeration. But the automats had kept up their productions and the things there were still fresh. He wondered at that, but he guessed, even now, things had to do what they did. At least until the autovolts remade their own kind of automats, these machines would keep doing what they'd been made to do. It was a perfect world but no one was left to live in it.

They stocked up on sandwiches and bread and milk. They got fresh apples from the machine and, for a treat, two cold sodas that they drank right there in the muggy summer heat.

He knew they'd see one soon, and they did. The autovolt came down the avenue at a jog, the rubber soles of its treads making the approach almost silent. The whine of the servos in its joints gave some advanced warning.

Jogger had seen a good amount of combat. Its gun was empty and retracted, the knife hand instead at the ready. The smooth plastic of its outer shell was scuffed and marred in places where bullets had struck or desperation had given way to hand-to-hand fighting. Through the transparent plastic and rubberized shell, Kerion could see the perfect inner mechanisms clicking like a timepiece. His father had had a transparent watch. It seemed just the same; its pieces carefully selected, its working no less miraculous for it.

Barry gripped his arm and pressed in behind him. "Dad?"

"Just like before. Just like every time. Don't worry, Barry."

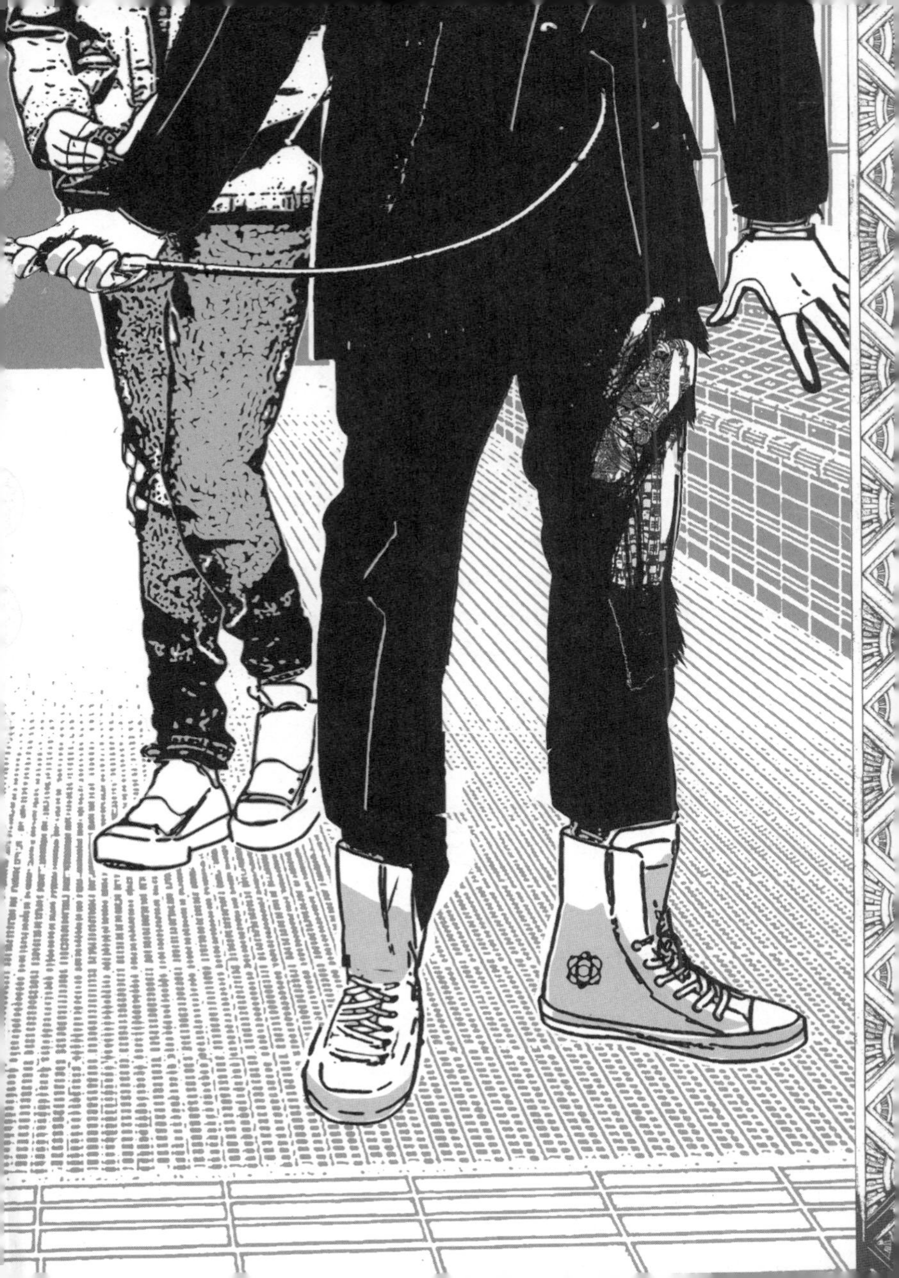

Jogger came up and politely identified itself.

"I am Unit 98302359-720. Identify yourself."

"I am Unit 8347-34."

"Incorrect. You are a human occupant."

Kerion looked at the knife hand. There was a nick in the blade.

"Exchange to verify," Kerion said.

"Exchange to verify," Unit 98302359-720 said.

Kerion lifted his shirt, exposing the flechette machine pistol tucked into his belt. He took the retracted power cable by its grip, extending it towards the autovolt. The autovolt took it and inserted it into its own port, then extended its own cable to Kerion, who took the cable and plugged it into place. His hands were sweating.

"Ident Verified 8347-34. Disconnect."

"No," Kerion said. He adjusted a knob on his abdomen under his shirt. Sparks flew inside the autovolt, and the humanoid figure shuddered for a moment, then slowly tilted forward. Kerion caught the heavy body and braced against it.

"Overloadoverloadoverloadoverloadoverload," Unit 98302359-720 said.

"Die," Kerion whispered to its smooth plastic face, then disconnected the cables—first the autovolt's, then his.

"Does it hurt them, Dad?" Barry asked.

"I hope so."

"You tell me not to be cruel."

"I do. I do. I'm sorry. It doesn't hurt them because they aren't alive. Finish your soda, then help me turn it over. I want to get its radio. Then we need to get back. I'm low."

//8347-34//

In the seventh war Kerion had lost his legs, a lung, a liver and his kidneys. His prosthetics were a miracle then, but he had hated them. He was no longer whole, and his wife's love was only a word; his identity was tested, thin. He had to charge on a trickler for two hours a day to stay at full power. Without it, he would die when his organs switched off. He had seven hours of battery. There was a design flaw that allowed the battery cell to dump its charge while in a power/data exchange. Very dangerous. He had been recalled for a switch-out last year but had decided to wait until after Christmas. Sometimes the recovery process took longer than the army doctors said it would, and he had been ashamed to pass the holidays in a wheelchair.

He had hated being automatic when the autovolts had come and the killing started. People would spot his chassis, where printed on his chest, small but ever-present, was a reminder that he was not just himself any longer. *Unit 8347-34.* He had hated his rebuilt body, had lost his wife but saved his son because of it.

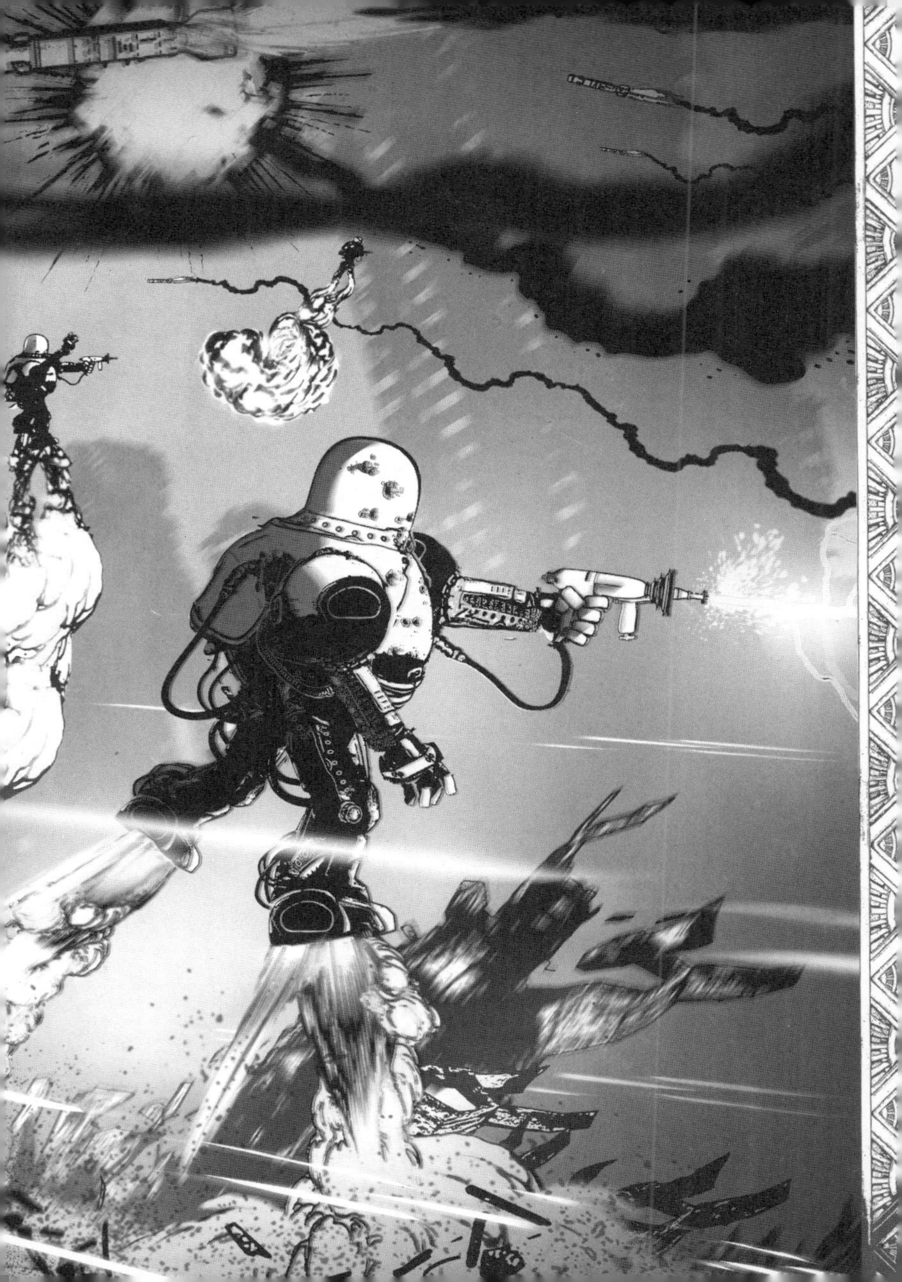

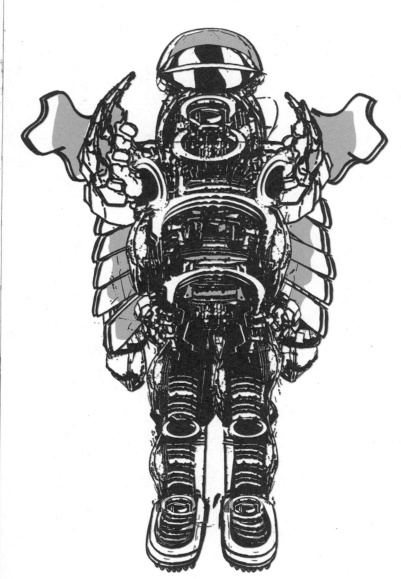

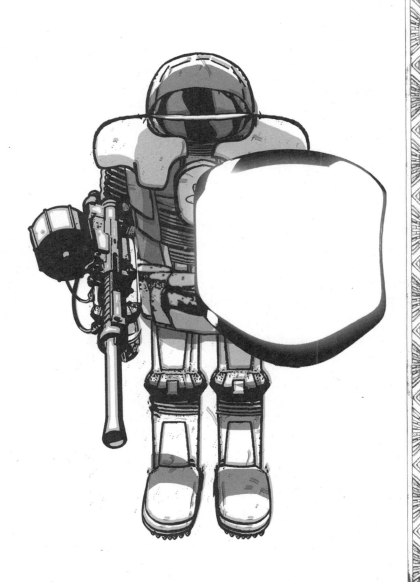

//LASAGNA//

"Where were you?" Kerion asked once Barry's sudden
intake of breath heralded his return from the nostalgic
trickle of the DayDreamer.

They were both seated on the floor of the SpinWin
Laundry Centre in their underwear. The folding machine
hummed behind them and the smell of warm lilac-scented
laundry wafted. At the rear of the SpinWin, a set of autorobs were bringing in the evening loads from uptown.
They took care of the sheets and linens of twenty hotels on
a schedule, guests or not, it appeared. The slender limbs
of the loading autorobs filled the washers one at a time.

Barry was staring at him.

"What is it?"

"You look so different."

"What?"

"You… It's just that… you were there, and here you
look—"

Kerion knew, his beard was in thick and tangled, his
hair was a shaggy mess.

"I know, it's hard to snap it all back into place when that thing really works. Where were you?"

"I was playing with the radio-controlled train set. The day Mom decided to get a dog. You were there. We laughed so hard. Now you try it."

Kerion lifted the Pleasant Pill pack, only a few left.

"Not tonight for me," he said. "Do you want some more lasagna?"

"No thank you. You tired?"

"Nope."

"Can we go get haircuts?"

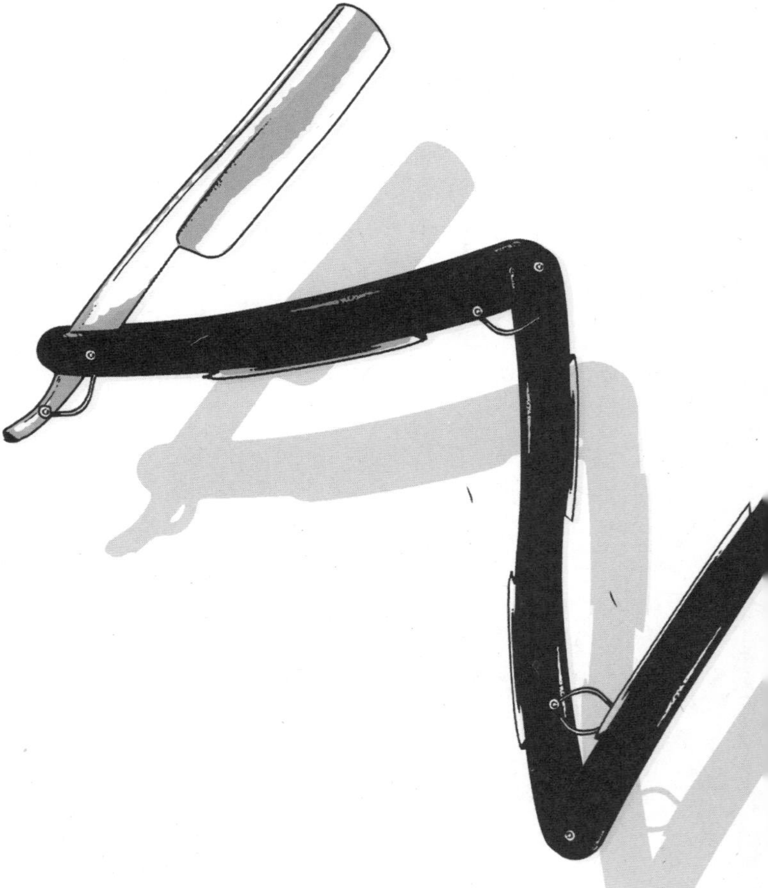

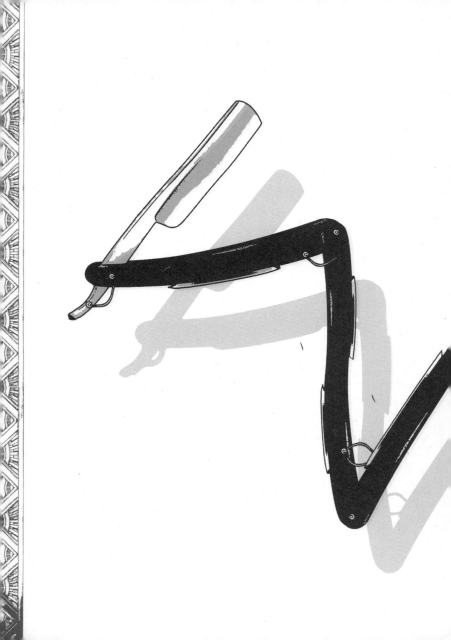

//BARBERSTOP//

Kerion and Barry sat in the chairs and the selection videos started to play on the little chrome armrest TVs of the TrimStar BarberStop. Barry pressed his button with a beep and a little dome descended with a click. Kerion considered his choice. There was a little black button and if he pressed it, the chair would tilt back and the autorob would trim his beard then lather him for an 'old fashioned straight razor shave.' Before, he had always punched that button with a confident click. Now he hesitated. He beeped the console and the autorob got to work with the hair foam on his face, removing the bristles the modern way, with seafoam green dissolvent on his beard and the vacuum electric trimmers extended to whisk away his unwanted locks.

"You look good, Dad," Barry said when their chairs tilted upright to deposit them standing at the mirrors.

"Like you remember?"

"Close."

Kerion frowned.

"You just look more like, 'you' you know?"

"I feel more like me too."

They deposited their coins, flipped the green switches to indicate they were happy with the service. Barry stood, holding an unused coin. The bronze token glinted as he twisted it in his hand.

"You okay?"

"Dad, why do we *pay*?"

"Because the autorobs won't work without it, and if we leave without paying we can't come back."

"But everything costs the same."

"Yes, one coin per item or use, just like Before."

Kerion lifted his back from the counter and took his jacket from the hook. He looked at himself in the wall mirror again and for a moment forgot that it wasn't Before, that he wouldn't step into the next podcar and flit off to work down the turbo tube.

They left the BarberStop and walked into the street. The lights were on and the calming music of the strollway murmured in the breeze. They walked beside the moving walkway, careful not to tread on it. Kerion had no direct evidence that the walkways called the autovolts, but twice using them had lead them to a confrontation. He knew that powering up an empty house brought them at once, but using the autoservices didn't seem to bring them, he supposed because they were all powered up and doing their various functions whether people were there or not. The watchmaker was gone but the whole grand affair was ticking away.

"But, Dad?"

"Yeah?"

"Why does everything cost the same. Like, a pair of shoes and a pie aren't useful the same amount?"

"Before the Automatic Age, things did all cost different amounts. But once Standardization took over, well, it didn't seem fair to value things differently because everyone had enough. Once labour wage became obsolete—"

"I don't understand."

"Look." Kerion waved his hand at an ice cream cart that had turned down the road. It lit up, played its music happily and wheeled up beside them. Kerion reached into his pocket and pulled out a coin. "It's tradition to pay for things. It made people of the older generations feel guilty to just take and take. As if they hadn't earned it." Kerion slotted the coin and the hatch popped open. The cold air puffed out. He reached in and took out an ice cream cone, peeled the paper top off and handed it to Barry.

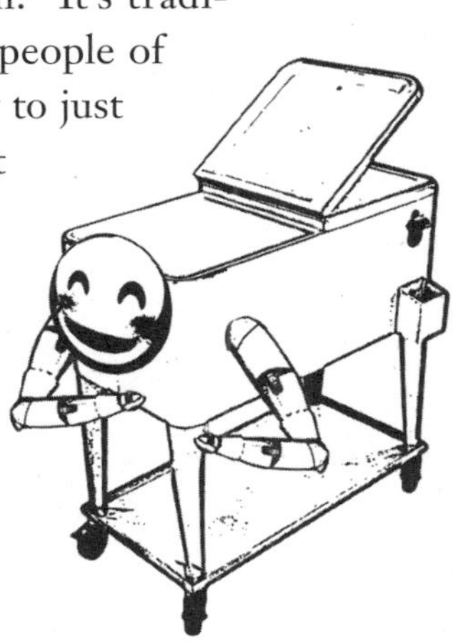

"I don't want it. Sorry, Dad."

Kerion put it in the waste slot, then the ice cream car wheeled off on a fruitless search for summer revellers.

"Where do the coins come from?"

"Well that's a tradition too. Money used to be a measure of merit given to people for their work. If you worked hard sometimes you could get more. The more money you had, the more comfortable your life."

"But then, if you got comfortable from working, you could never rest? So you could never be comfortable, not really."

Kerion knelt and took Barry's hands.

"I'll keep you safe."

Barry was startled and kept on, "What happened when everyone stopped really paying for things?"

"We're paying for it now, I guess," Kerion said.

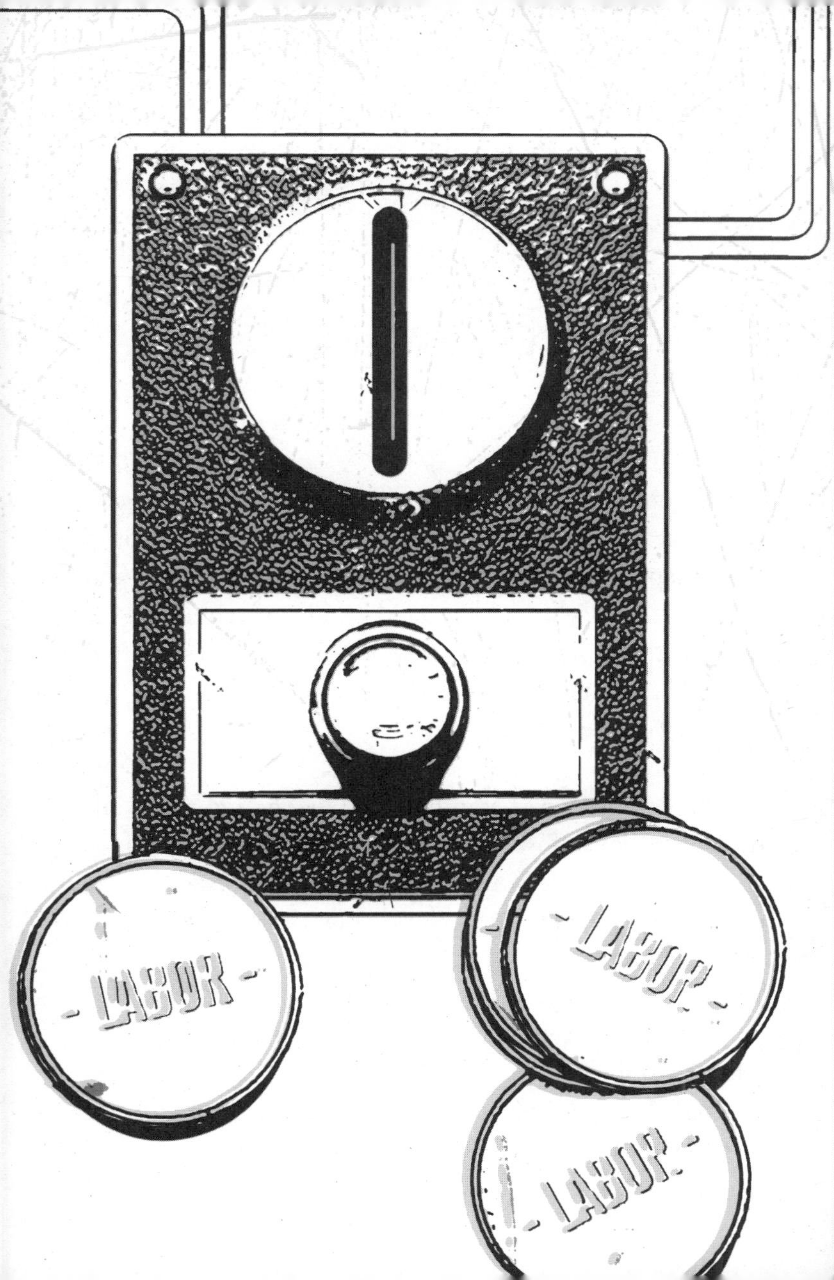
LABOR
LABOR
LABOR

//YELLOWHEAD//

They crouched behind a merry-go-round near the edge of the park. It went round and round, rockets and unicorns, waving spacemen and princesses, flapping butterflies and dragons. Music chimed. Beside the stairs, in a brass basket labelled LOST AND FOUND, a dozen rain-soiled stuffed animals were neatly arranged.

"Do you see it?"

"Yes."

The autovolt was standing still on the moving walk. Its clear body allowed the overhead lights to cast odd shadows within it. Somewhere on its mission, someone or something had poured a large quantity of yellow paint over its head.

"It's going to go right past. Don't worry."

And it did. Yellowhead slipped silently along within a few dozen meters of them. Then a cotton candy cart spotted them, chimed, whirled to life and said *"I've got the sweet things to sweeten your summer day!"*

The autovolt turned its head and began to walk backwards on the moving walk. The walkway's pace halted its progression, it bobbed there, walking in place, staring in their direction with its dandelion paint-shrouded visage.

"It sees us. Stay here and I'll—"

"YOU!"

The shout made Kerion flinch. He looked around for its source behind him.

"YOU!"

"Barry stay down and stay there."

"Dad!"

"YOU!" louder.

Yellowhead stepped off of the pathway and strode toward Kerion. It raised its arm. A thin barrel extended, and there was the sound of a shot, thunderous, then Yellowhead's torso burst away, leaving its arms and head to dangle from the smoking ruins of its legs.

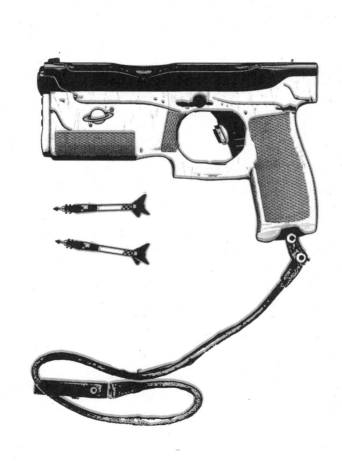

//ASTRO-NOT//

The man had crooked glasses with clear frames, his shirt was pressed, his pants pleats were perfect, but both the shirt and slacks had dark stains that laundering had not removed.

"You a Delta?" he said.

"What?" Kerion said.

"Drop your weapon," the stranger said. When he spoke to Kerion, he gestured with one hand that quivered with a slight tremor. In his other he held a chrome rocket pistol on a long leather strap with a fastener at one end: an astrojumper's weapon. The secure strap was meant to clasp to the outside of a Zero G flight suit. Here it looked like a dog leash dragging on the ground.

"Drop your weapon," the stranger said again, and Kerion took the flechette machine pistol from his belt and placed it slowly on the ground. Kerion's arm had three pieces of Yellowhead's transparent shell sunk in it, the wounds around the shrapnel oozed.

"I recognize you."

"No you don't."

Kerion shook his head. His haircut and an autoshave had returned him to the picture perfect vision of the past.

"Sure I do," He raised his hands in a flourish, framing an imaginary marquee. "Hero of the Seventh War! I saw your face on the newsreels. Before. Didn't know I was sharing the neighborhood with a bonafide 7W hero."

"We weren't heroes, just what was left over. It was easier to give us all medals and three minutes of fame than admit to the catastrophe of it all."

Barry had never heard his father talk about the war to any adult. The stranger didn't seem to really listen though. Didn't know the rarity of the topic of conversation. He titled his head conspiratorially, shifting his glasses. There was sweat in his eyes again and he blinked them but never wiped it away. He hissed a bit when he spoke. "They are like ants, I think. Exchanging information in a way that can't be trusted to send over radio. They serve the Current. It's their god." The stranger blinked both eyes repeatedly. "But we can fight them. A resistance. We'll resist. We'll fight. I just need soldiers, people to train. Young people." The stranger was staring at Barry.

"Barry, we have to go." Kerion stepped directly in front of his son.

"No. Stay with me, sir. We can fight them. Take back this suburb."

"You're right, they do connect to exchange info. But when they're damaged, like the one you just shot up, they radio for help. That little square box hanging there, that's the radio. We need to get out of here. Barry, come here. Hold my hand. We are leaving."

"No. Stay with me, sir. We can fight them. Take back this suburb. You're a hero. I'm a hero. I'm an astronaut! I'm a Delta! We're the exception! We're exceptional!"

"Come on, Barry."

"No," the stranger said. He alternated pointing the rocket pistol at each of them and was sweaty and wide eyed, grinding his teeth even as he grinned. He shoved Kerion back. "You stay right there." Then the stranger's face knotted as he stared at the place he had touched Kerion. His eyes went wider, and then he grabbed at Kerion, pointing the weapon at his face. The stranger's hand felt around on the prosthesis chassis. He seized Kerion and pushed up his shirt.

"You're one of them."

"No."

"You're one of them." The stranger tore at Kerion's shirt and pressed the gun to his chest.

"No. Just wait. Let my son go."

"He's one, too. You're them." He levelled the pistol at Barry. "Ohhhhh. I *get* it. Look like us now to get the rest! I get it—but you won't get me!"

In the war, after a while, you just did it. There was no triumph in the war. But here Kerion felt the guilt of triumph when he pushed up the barrel and pinioned it over, twisting the strap to trap the stranger's arm. He put the knife up under the stranger's chin all the way in until his closed hand was snug under the jaw. Then he let it go as the dead man fell backward to the ground.

"We have to go now, Barry. Quick as we can."

Kerion took the weapon, checked it. Two shots. A choice he rejected. He put the rocket pistol in his pack, then picked up the machine pistol and tucked it back into his belt.

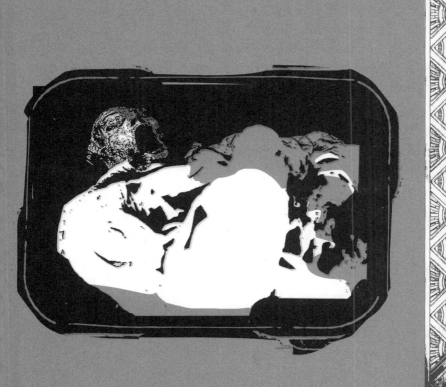

//FAULT//

When Kerion removed the DayDreamer contacts he saw that Barry was examining the single extra magazine of flechette ammunition. There was an elegance in how the thing was folded and compressed, like a origami puzzle of frozen metal.

"What did you DayDream?" Barry asked.

"New Year's."

"New Year's is fun."

"Not last year."

"Oh."

"It's okay."

"Sorry."

"It's not your fault. I wanted to. Maybe it's broken?"

"It worked for me."

"Maybe I am broken," Kerion said. He looked down at loops of the power cable that was plugged in under his shirt.

Barry hugged him and they slumped down on the booth seat of the restaurant.

"You're my dad."

//LEAFGLASS//

They sat down under the canopy of elms. The summer sun reached for them, but the little green space had a covered picnic bench.

"What do you think, Dad?"

"I think it could be a great find. We'll need to wait until dark and see."

Across a bridge that spanned an artificial creek was a nice little main-floor condominium. It had a lovely pool and indoor gym, a carpod platform right outside the door and a moving sidewalk to the park nearby. It was furnished in sweeping mahogany polygonal shapes and memory foam. The light fixtures rose like flowers from the floor stems. There was a big library of old books that they could see through the glass. Real books, like the fairy tale book in Barry's bag, didn't require any vidscreen access. Kerion was becoming increasingly suspicious of vidscreen time; he was sure that it would become an obvious way for the autovolts to find the location of curious humans.

"Books are secrets now," Kerion had said when they had spotted the condominium's treasures.

They couldn't just go in. They had to watch the automatics and robs first. During the day, nearly everything they needed worked by pulling energy from the sun's rays. Photovoltaic. Solar Power. But at night the things they used drew power from the Grid. When they used power at night outside of a regular cycle it seemed to bring the autovolts. It wasn't always the case. But somewhere an autovolt in a relay station would see the tiny spike in power use and walk to the closest autovolt to pass on the message. It would in turn pass the message to the next closest until it reached the autovolt assigned to their sector. In his mind that seemed slow, but it really wasn't. Though it had been a difficult theory to test.

"Why don't they use the radio for that?" Barry had asked.

"It seems like they were designed to be careful of transmission. An enemy could listen or send false information. But they also don't rely on satellites I guess. A friend of mine told me they were developed for extra-terran operations. Attacking enemy dome cities on Venus."

"Do we have enemies on Venus?"

"No. Now everyone left is on their own side."

So Kerion and Barry often waited and watched a new place for a full day to see what was already on, things they could use without changing the grid reading of a dwelling too dramatically. Turned a few things off then plugged in a few others. If too many things turned on because they were there, that brought the autovolts for sure. They could use things as they pleased during the day so long at that little Solar symbol was on the power relay. They didn't go into any of the old buildings that didn't have that symbol if they could help it. Some of the systems were activated automatically, by motion. The lights would come up, music would play, and dinner would begin cooking.

"So if they collect power like trees, what part works like the leaves?" Barry asked.

"It's the glass. The glass collects the solar power, which is partially why there is so much of it in the design of these newer buildings."

They watched hungrily as the auto kitchen made a pot roast, cut the vegetables, roasted them in oil, set the table, poured wine into two wide-mouthed glasses, juice into a tumbler, then after an hour cleared the table, dumping the lot into the composting chute.

Kerion took out some canned peaches and a loaf of bakery bread. Nothing wrong with it. Barry seldom went hungry as the vending machines and automats had food aplenty. Restocked as soon as they came to their best before dates. But there was no substitute for a fully home-cooked meal.

It occurred to Barry, as it must have occurred to the autovolts, that if you wanted to get rid of people, turning everything off for a year would probably do it. Starve out the human race with minimal fuss. But maybe some part of their program was to leave things better than they found them. If the grid was turned off for a year things would break down. An army of autorobs would be needed to fix it up again. Was it easier to just send your hunters to look carefully door to door? It took time, Barry guessed. But what was time to a robot after all?

Sometimes Kerion and Barry would come upon a great reconstruction project. Dozerobs fleets clearing wreckage and debris with systematic precision. Pouring new piles or printing new dwellings. The destruction wrought by the human resistance had accelerated the urban planning department's schedule. Once the site of the fighting was scooped out, new, more modern dwellings were erected efficiently.

Barry had noticed an escalation in the ad competition for the new dwellings too. Enticements and beep attention ads on every vid screen they passed blinked information about the new habitations. It hinted at a sort of desperation in the Housing Department, which, made for making places for humans to live, suddenly found itself without any clientele. Barry wondered if an automatic system could feel shame when no one showed up to use the thing it had made. Was its desire to do the thing leveraged by a programmed pride or desire to please the user?

The new buildings were very dangerous now because all the ultra-modern construction had hermetic seals built in. They would snap shut like a Venus flytrap and digest you slowly with their central heating and cooling units. Maybe there were people somewhere in some of these new places, content to live within the sealed apartments, never able to leave but never wanting to.

"It's not all voice connected. Thankfully, the architects had that much sense. But a lot of it talks to each other in certain ways I think. They are on a different mission now. Not just hunt and kill, but systematic, careful. They assign autovolts to watch and learn. Machines can be slow to learn, but once they learn, they act on success without delay."

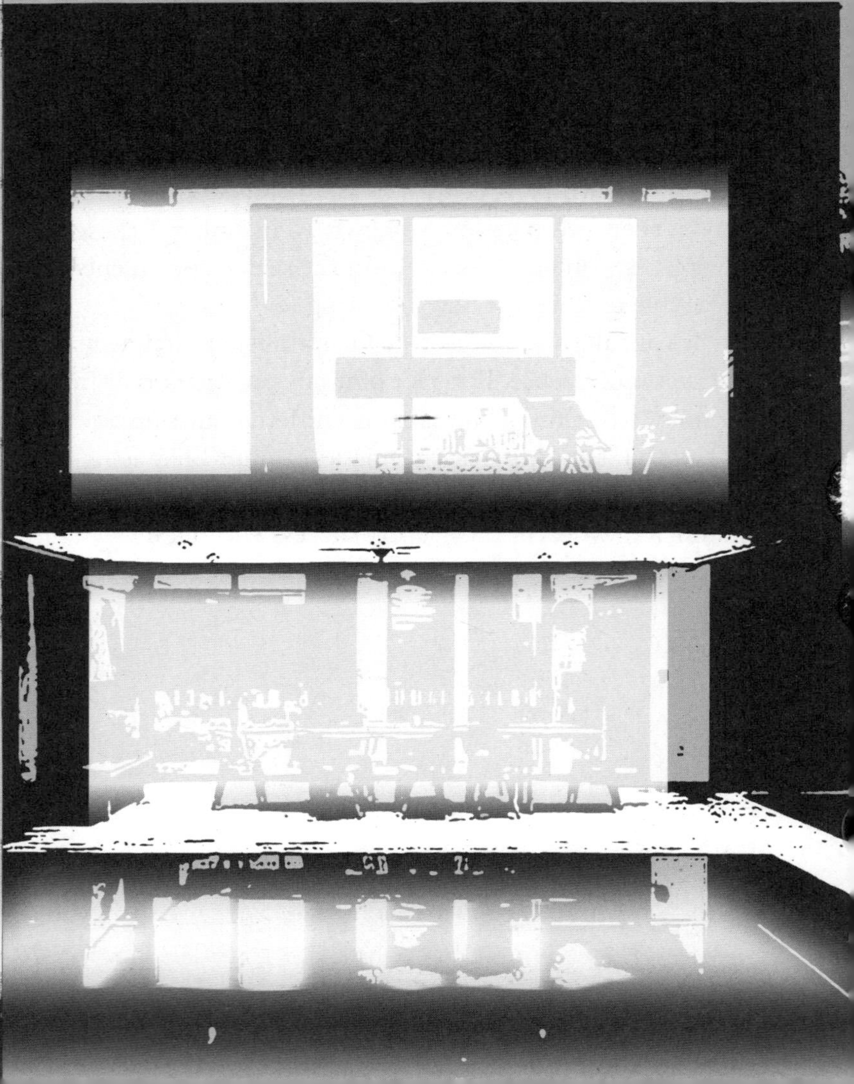

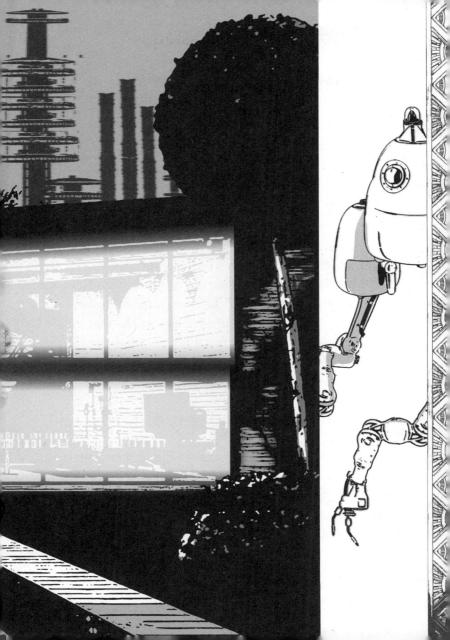

//EMPTYBOOKSHELF//

Kerion determined that the house was safe enough to enter, which they did the next day at lunch time.

They both went straight to the bookshelf. Kerion reached for the blue spine of the *Vacuum Diode Engineering*. It was fake. Just a facsimile of a book spine that opened to reveal alcoholic drinks in crystal bottles.

Barry could tell how disappointed his dad was. He checked every book.

"A cruel joke," Kerion said.

They ate the fresh mixed green salad the kitchen had prepared, then left.

The autovolt was crossing the bridge as they came out. Whether it was something they had triggered that brought it or if it was just on a patrol they didn't know. They had been very careful, but they had missed something and there it was. As it came closer to them, Barry saw that its hands were smeared with fresh blood.

"Get behind me."

"I know. Okay."

"I am Unit 97812359-612. Identify yourself."

"I am Unit 8347-34," Kerion said.

"Incorrect. You are a human occupant."

"Exchange to verify," Kerion said.

"Exchange to verify," Redhands said.

Kerion pulled the cord free, but it caught on something internally for a moment, then came free, unspooling normally as the autovolt traded cables.

"Ident Verified 8347-34. Disconnect."

Kerion didn't, and again sent the surge of power from his battery system into the delicate heart of the autovolt. It teetered on depowered legs and stumbled backwards, one foot misstepping on the edge of the creek. It twisted and fell in, toppling over and dragging Kerion, still attached and off balance, into the water.

It was startling, but the water wasn't deep nor the current strong. Kerion was soaking to the waist but unhurt.

"It's okay. I'm okay."

Barry moved about on the edge of the creek uncertain as to what to do.

"I just need to turn it over so I can detach. It's jammed up and tangled on its arm."

Barry looked very concerned.

"Hey," Kerion said.

"What?"

"It's fine," then he splashed Barry with the cool clean water of the creek.

They both laughed.

Then Barry saw Scratches. Whatever had befallen this new autovolt, it had covered the normally glass-smooth polish of its outer covering in thick scratches. It rounded the condominum's pool.

Barry ran to the front door of the condo, grabbed the lamp in the entryway, ran back and jumped into the water beside his father. Kerion used the lamp as a lever to flip the autovolt while Barry struggled to untangle the cables.

As soon as they were free they were out of the creek and running.

Kerion could feel his legs slowing, powersave mode gearing down his run. They made it to the park. Looking back, they saw Scratches had begun a steady running pace to overtake them.

"I...Barry, I..." Kerion didn't have the charge he needed. "I made a mistake somehow. I d-didn't—"

"I know you don't have the charge. Use the rocket pistol," Barry said.

"I've never fired one, but I think if I use it too close it could hurt us. If I shoot and miss it'll use that rifle and we're"—Kerion paused. "It's better for me to stick with the flinger. I've had more practice with it."

Barry looked at the flechette pistol, the flinger. It wasn't that effective against the autovolts since it had been designed to kill human soldiers and didn't have much of what his father called 'stopping power'. You had to catch the autovolt in close range and keep shooting until the combined barrage allowed something to penetrate that smooth surface.

Scratches had slowed as he reached the soft green lawn of the park. A bronze statue of the Founder of Genetic Standardization stood on a slight dias, hands on hips, his Martian uniform rendered in metal, crisp and angular. They dodged around it, putting it between Scratches and them.

"I can get him when he's close," Kerion said reaching into his bag and withdrawing the flechette pistol.

"It's too dangerous," Barry said, "He'll—" Then he had a sudden insight. A desperate plan. He looked up and caught his father in the intensity of his stare, "Dad, I'll tell him what I am."

"It's too dangerous."

"It's too late to argue, Dad."

Scratches was there, looming.

"I am Unit 57772659-321. Identify yourself."

"I am Unit 8347-34," Kerion said rising slowly.

"Incorrect. You are a human occupant."

"Exchange to verify," Kerion said.

"Exchange to verify," Scratches said.

With still wet hands, Kerion passed his cable to the autovolt. He hoped the tremble in his hand would not cause him to drop it.

"Ident Verified 8347-34. Disconnect."

Then to Barry it said, "I am Unit 57772659-321. Identify yourself."

"I am *so* sick of you." Barry said.

The autovolt raised the rifle at the third syllable, and Barry started to run even as he said it. He ducked left of the autovolt, which pivoted smoothly, tracking him as he went. It could sight him easily at 500 meters with the rifle. Only a protocol politeness prevented the autovolts from shooting them on sight and mandated an escalation from close-quarter killing to long range. But once identified there was no hiding from the rifles. They had seen many try.

The autovolt was just shouldering its rifle when Kerion shot it in head with the flechette pistol. The supersonic slivers chipped away the face then started ripping the head apart in a staccato beat. The projectiles had made tiny holes as they entered and dragged out the inner mechanisms in high speed blossoms as they exited the head. Beyond the autovolt, the glass edifice of the office block shattered and cascaded into the walking path. The autovolt fired its rifle. The pop flash made Kerion flinch, it was so close. Barry screamed, and Kerion fell back, his legs' auto-reflexers too slow and his balance still affected by powerloss.

The headless autovolt was still pointing and firing with purpose and care. Kerion couldn't look until the next shot reminded him that if the autovolt was still shooting, then it had missed Barry.

Barry was hiding behind the statue. Scratches stalked forward, headless, took measured shots that struck the statue in vital areas and cause it to ring like a bell. Pwang! and the metal head had a divot, Pwang! and the chest caved in. It did not see that Barry crouched behind the dias.

"Stay there!" Kerion called.

Kerion fumbled for the rocket pistol, pointed and fired. Tried to fire. It didn't work. Nothing.

Kerion snarled and tossed the weapon.

He flung open his pack for the last flechette magazine. It was gone. It was in Barry's pack.

The autovolt ran out of ammunition and carefully placed the rifle on the ground. The knife flipped out of its forearm and it began to walk forward.

"Arrrrrrrrrrrgggggggg." Kerion screamed as he strained to drag his inert lower half.

Barry stood when the shooting stopped. He looked at his father, then at Scratches. The autovolt struck the statue with the knife in a careful draw upward through the place the femoral artery in the thigh would have been if the target had not been made of bronze.

Crawling forward, dragging the deadweight of his lower half, Kerion begged the autovolt to turn, to come for him, to leave his son alone. But it ignored him because it saw Kerion as a fellow autovolt.

Barry stepped back from the statue of the Honoured Genetic Pioneer and the autovolt saw him again. It lunged and he ran.

Kerion was left screaming as his son ran off while a machine designed to kill humans chased Barry out of the park.

//REVOLVING//

"It didn't have bullets or a head," Barry said.

Barry uncoiled extension cords he had bought from a hobby store two blocks away.

"I made it chase me up to the overlook level. Remember where we climbed between the two balconies?"

"I remember."

"Well, I ran there, it got caught up in the rotating door, which bought me some time. I jumped across and waited on the balcony. It came running and crash, fell into the freeway under the overlook."

"Did it—"

"SMASH!" Barry said, then, "Here. Plug in. Quick." There was a quiver in the sincerity of his positivity, but the exhilaration was real.

Kerion plugged in.

Barry didn't expand his story, didn't tell his father about how the autovolt had grabbed hold of his sleeve just as he jumped into the revolving door. How he had undone his jacket and abandoned it to escape its grasp. He didn't tell his dad about how, crying and sweat slick, he had nearly fallen while climbing to the glass rail of the balcony, so that he could jump, just in time, as the autovolt crashed through the partition and fell while he clutched desperately to the balcony edge.

"I lost my jacket though," was all he said.

Kerion seized him. A hand on each side of his head. He pushed his forehead to his son's.

In a low voice he said, "I'm proud of you."

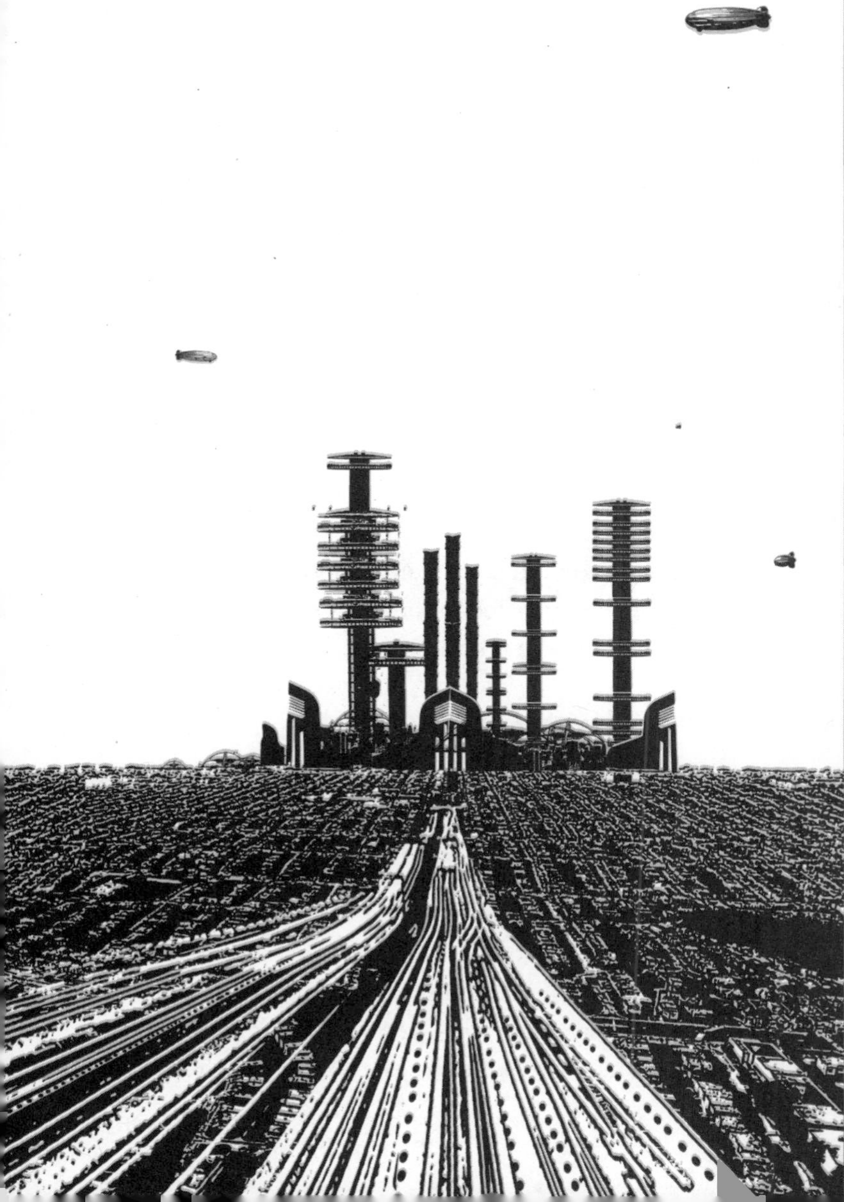

//REVOLVINGCOSMOS//

"You said we need to stay in the suburbs. Away from the city stacks."

"I did. But that was months ago. It should be empty now."

"What do you mean?"

"The autovolts are efficient. They went where the people were. They started in the city stacks. Which means people won't be there now. But that's not really why we're going."

"Why are we going?"

"It's your birthday tomorrow."

"You mean…?" Barry smiled, sudden and genuine.

"Yep."

The suburbs gave way to the city. The city proper sloped toward the stacks. At the top of the city stacks was the Revolving Cosmos Automat. It was a trick to get there using only the escalators and the stairs. It took them into the next day and night. Kerion was afraid to use the pneumatic lifts. Too easy to be captured. They didn't meet a single autovolt along the way. They didn't even see one. They avoided those newer hermetically sealed buildings. Most had been locked tight during Last Christmas and Kerion was afraid of what Barry might see pressed against the breakproof glass.

They reached The Revolving Cosmos Automat just before midnight, but it was still technically Barry's birthday so the promise was kept. They slept in the booths until sunrise. The Revolving Cosmos Automat was a spinning automat set like a crown on top of the highest stack. The great green-grey and blue checkerboard of perfect urban planning stretched in all directions.

"How high up are we?"

"Over two kilometers, I should think."

"Can I use the 'scopes?!"

"Sure." Kerion dug in his pocket and pulled out a handful of coins. "Can I join you, kiddo?"

"Yeah, Dad. That's swell!"

Barry put in a coin and got up into the chair of the Superscope apparatus. The machine was as large as a coin-operated vibrating rocket ride. There was a dome over it with open doors on each side, like the little helicopter rides at the fair. There was a yellow line around the Superscope that reminded people that the whole apparatus spun. Kerion climbed into a second apparatus a little way up the promenade. As Barry's chair spun and zoomed, he guided the view on the screen slowly up the buzzing freeway. He was slow and careful. The whisking cars he ignored. When the freeway was crosshatched by the five dozen magtube lines, he set the waypoint on the screen and looked up.

Barry plopped another coin in and shouted with glee. Kerion went to the automat counter. Part of it had been smashed to pieces. But all the debris had been swept and cleared and the sharp parts dutifully identified by bright orange tape. Everything broken here had been cleaned and cleared by the autorobs. Kerion dropped some coins into the menu then selected a hot turkey sandwich with mashed potatoes and peas. Would he like a refreshing beverage? Yes. A milkshake, please.

He passed the meal and some napkins to Barry in the Superscope.

"Thanks Dad, this is—"

"Your favourite. I know. You're welcome. Happy birthday." Kerion put the milkshake on the console. Beads of condensation pulled down into a ring on the chrome surface. Barry had selected the HIDE AND SEEK function on the Superscope and was hunting out architecture in the city. Kerion went back to work.

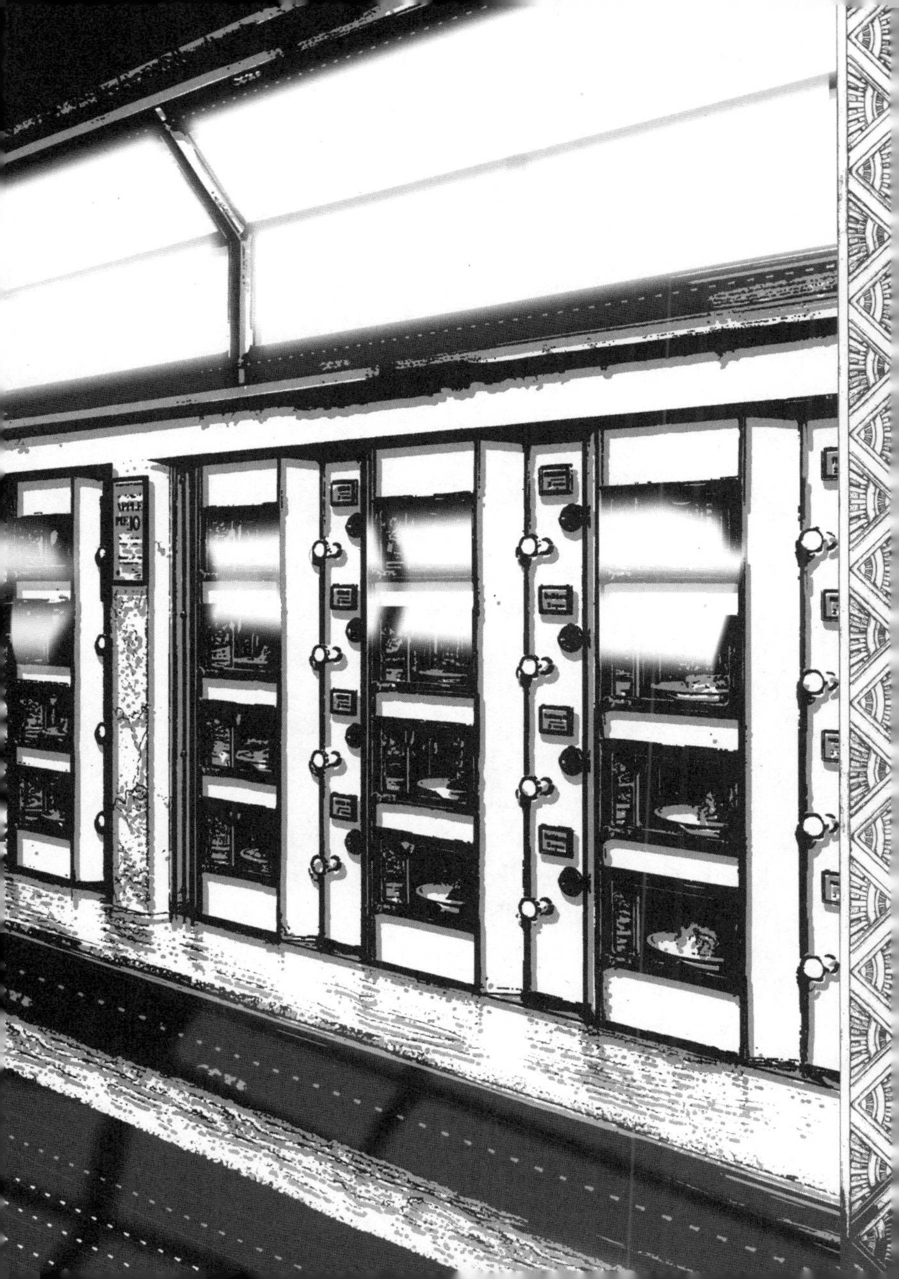
APPLE PIE 10

//NO ANSWER//

"Why do we have to leave?"

"You like it up here?"

"It's the best."

"Well, we can stay a few more days if you'd like. But then I think we need to move."

"Why?"

"It's something I said the day before your birthday. About the autovolts. They're efficient."

"Right, but you said they left."

"I know. But they are efficient and thorough and tireless. Eventually they'll come back for anyone they missed with their first effort."

"So we won't be here."

"Right."

"Can't you zap 'em? I know that last one was close, Dad but—"

"One at a time. When it's one autovolt and I have a day to recharge? Yes. Maybe even two at a time. But I'm afraid that things are changing. I'm afraid that when all the autovolts are done with one plan, they may come back as part of the next. Maybe that's what we saw by the statue."

"Oh."

"Don't be scared."

"Why not?"

Kerion didn't have an answer.

//HEARTHOLE//

It was Barry who spotted the next autovolt effort on the Superscope.

"What's that, Dad?"

"What's what?"

Kerion had bought a notebook from a vending machine two floors down and a pack of ballpoints. He bought nine short extension cords from an appliance window shop and had strung them together to draw his charge while he worked at the Superscope. He was making notes about the tube lines. Trying to find one they could reach on foot without a car. The tube trains were running as usual, and, unlike the cars, they had not been turned into moving coffins. The tubes carried the autovolts in batches across the country. They gathered on the platform in regiments, one or two at a time, before redeployment. It was the part of his plan that he wasn't sure about yet: getting on the platform, onto a train, and off again at the end of the line. He was making notes when Barry said:

"Woah. Dad, come see."

A wasp buzzed near Kerion's mouth curiously, he waved it away.

"All right, bud. Coming."

"I got the tracking to work. That is so cool."

It was two autovolts. They were zipping along up 203rd street on a wingless circular platform, like two lead soldiers on a tea saucer. The tracking lock on the Superscope kept them in frame. Both were heavily armed. Then, suddenly behind them, slightly out of focus, another flying platform crossed the frame.

"Zoom out."

They were looking at a growing procession. With every street they crossed, other discs fell into formation.

"Woah," Barry said.

"Right. Okay. Looks like our outing is over, sport." Kerion went over to his Superscope and started stuffing his things into his pack. "Grab your stuff and a snack from the 'mat if you want one for the walk down. Oh, and use the bathroom before we go."

"Dad."

"We need to keep off the moving walks and stairs too, I think—"

"Dad."

"—and grab a portable amp box, I was going to do that on the way up. I should have—"

"*Dad.*" Barry pointed.

"I am Unit 95320389-027. Identify yourself."

"I am Unit 38995320-072. Identify yourself."

Both of the autovolts stood at the entrance from the terrace into the automat. Both had rifles with bayonets attached. One had a scraped finish and a bullet hole above the place a heart would be. The other looked factory-new. Newone came toward Kerion while Hearthole moved toward Barry, who was trying to pull his pack on without making any sudden movements.

"I am Unit 8347-34," Kerion said to Newone.

"What do I say, Dad? Dad! *Dad*!"

Kerion stepped in front of Hearthole.

"I am Unit 8347-34," he said. Then, over his shoulder to Barry, "Don't run yet."

Hearthole paused. Newone paused, then together they said, "Incorrect. You are a human occupant."

"Exchange to verify," Kerion said, then motioned to Barry.

"Ex- Exchange to verify," Barry said.

Kerion passed his cable to Newone and motioned to the extension cord on the floor. Barry picked it up and passed it to Hearthole. Barry's hand was unsteady, but the autovolt took it with a quick motion.

"Incorrect connection," Heathole said.

Barry looked at his father with wide eyes. Kerion looked down to the machine pistol on his own belt. Barry shook his head.

"I love you, son," Kerion said.

"Ident Verified 8347-34. Disconnect," Newone said

Kerion drew the machine pistol. Hearthole lifted its rifle.

"No!" Barry shouted.

"Overloadoverloadoverloadoverloadoverload," Newone said.

Heathole was faster, just a fraction. The autovolts were always faster.

A single efficient shot from the autovolt, a burst of wildfire from Kerion's pistol on automatic, then a heart-beat of stillness as empty casings chimed on the ferrocrete on the terrace.

Kerion fell back against Newone. He wanted to scream "Run" to Barry, but all his breath was gone, stolen by the sputtering phosphor bullet from Hearthole's rifle. The rifle was in tatters after Kerion's barrage, so Hearthole dropped it and flipped his knife out from the wrist slot, turned its head, then its torso, then pivoted its legs away from Kerion, who fell to one knee clutching at the smol-dering hole in his abdomen. Barry scampered into the Superscope Kerion had been using and out the other side. Hearthole lunged after him much faster, stabbing for-ward. The blade stuck hard into Barry's backpack. Barry screamed and fell out the other side of the Superscope.

Kerion stood, then, with Newone's rifle, jabbed the bayonet into the socket groove of Hearthole's armpit. He reached into the Superscope and touched the first waypoint on the screen. The Superscope's apparatus spun into place, striking the autovolt and knocking it off balance and onto its back with the rifle's bayonet still wedged tight. Kerion kicked at the other flailing arm. He got his boot down on the delicate-looking wrist of the clutching hand and squeezed the rifle trigger. The shot popped the bayonet from the joint, and the chest of the clockwork simulacra flared a brilliant white as the phosphor round ignited inside it. Hearthole shook and spasmed on the terrace.

Its flailing limbs flipped Hearthole into the terrace glass, which shattered into tiny cubes. An alarm sounded, and ten vacuum and five sweeper autorobs spun to life from their wall alcoves.

Kerion staggered forward. Barry was sitting staring at him. Barry had found Kerion's pack beside the SuperScope and its contents were spilled out around the boy. Barry had the rocket pistol, huge and heavy in his tiny hands. Kerion swept up his pack and started putting things back inside.

Kerion, urgency in his body, but calm in his voice, said "You did great." Kerion put both hands around the chrome pistol and took it away slowly. "Next time, kiddo, you keep running though, okay."

"I thought you were gone."

"I'm right here."

Hearthole sat up.

"Go. Go. Go. Go. Go."

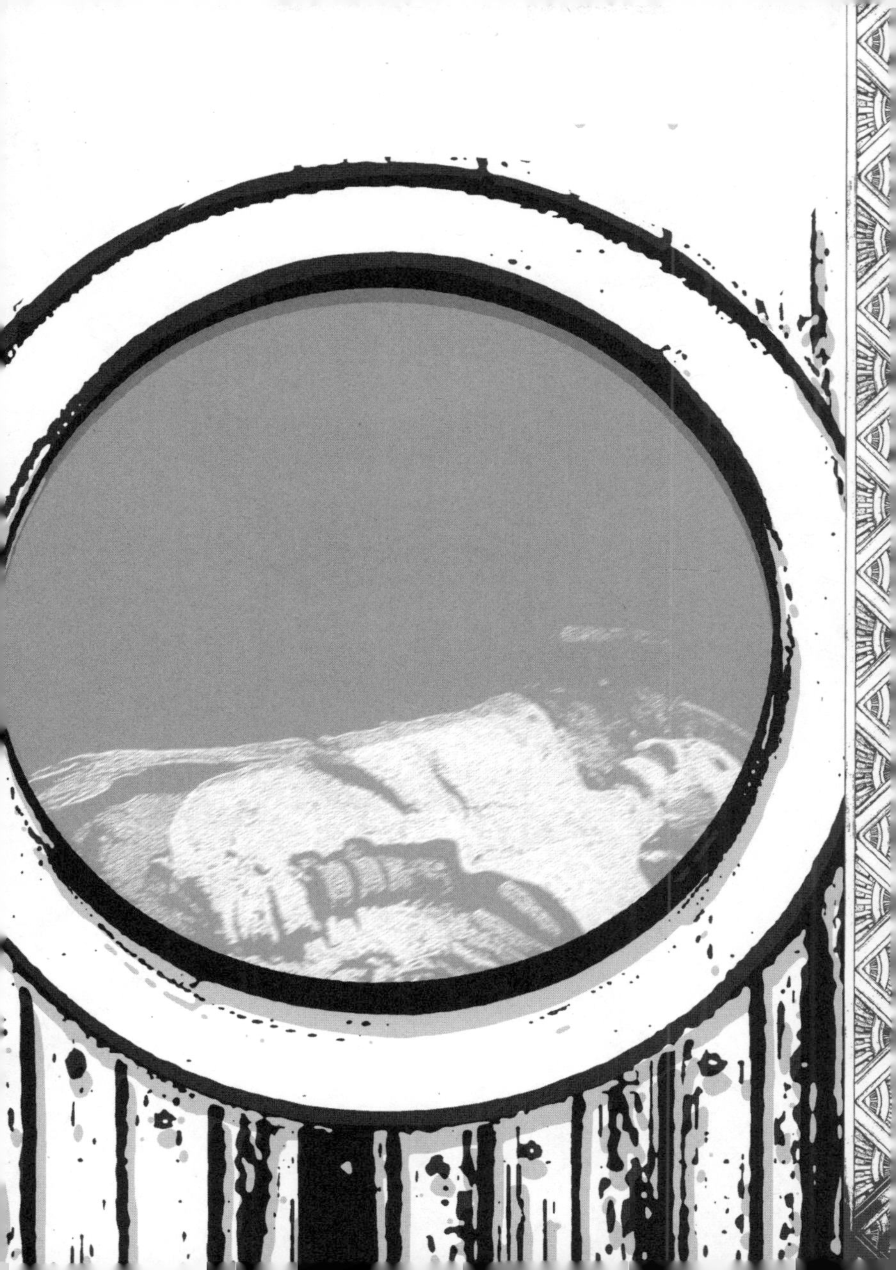

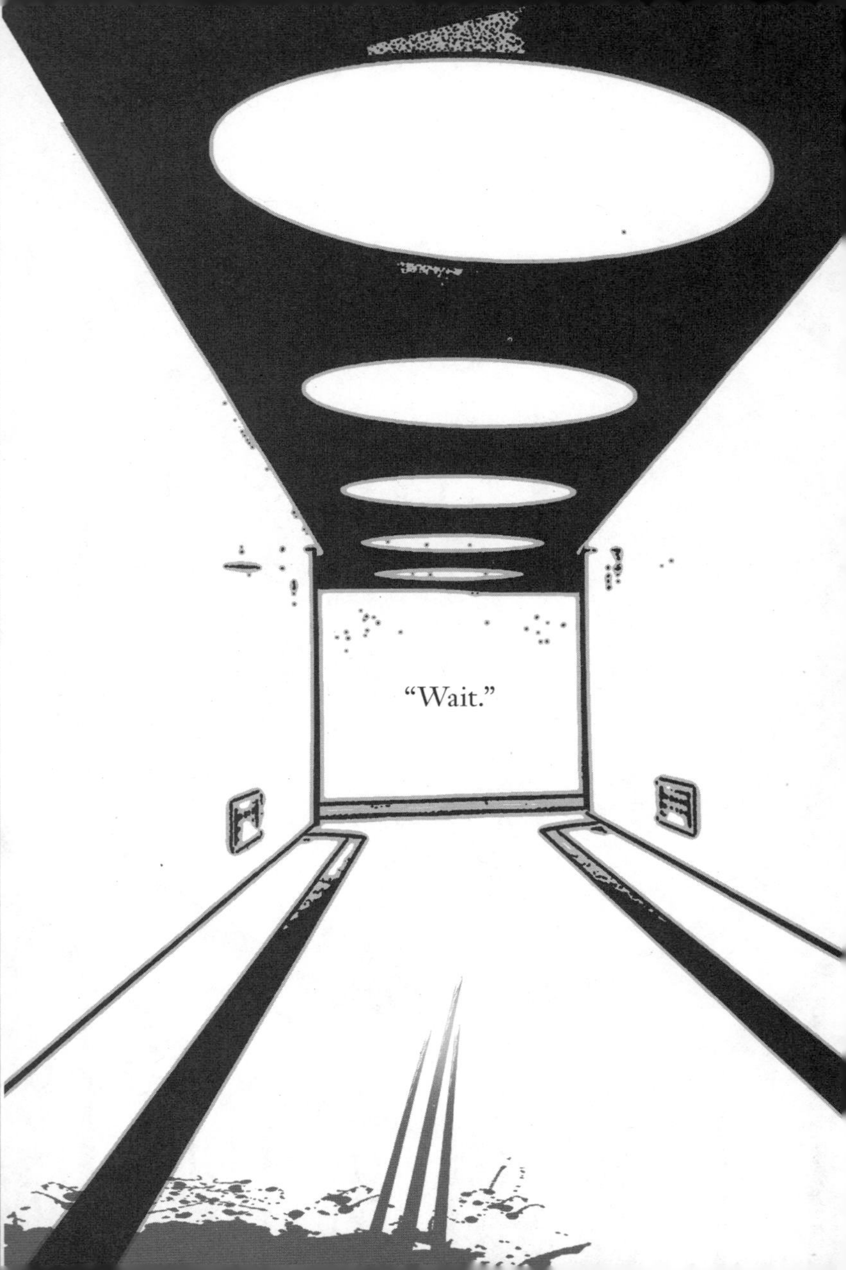
“Wait.”

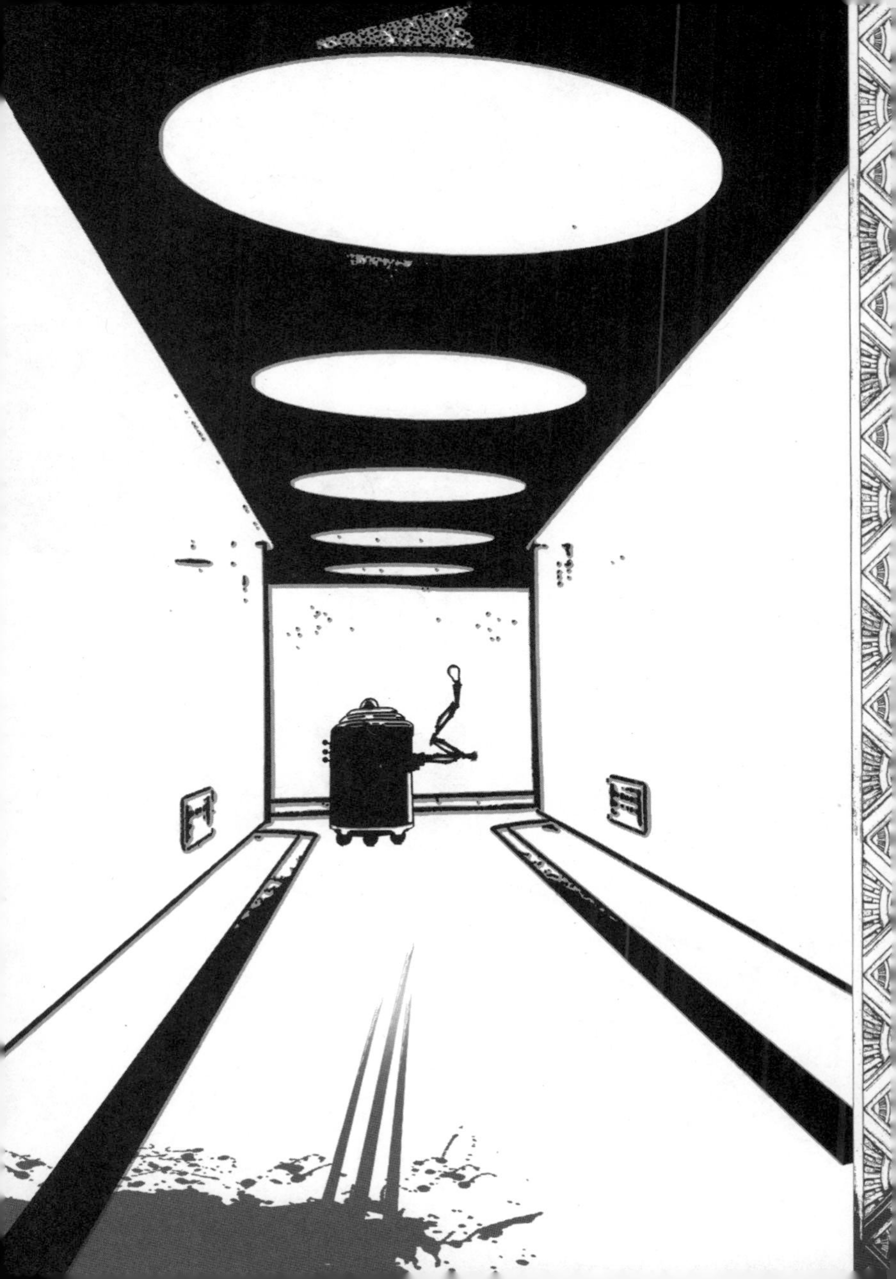

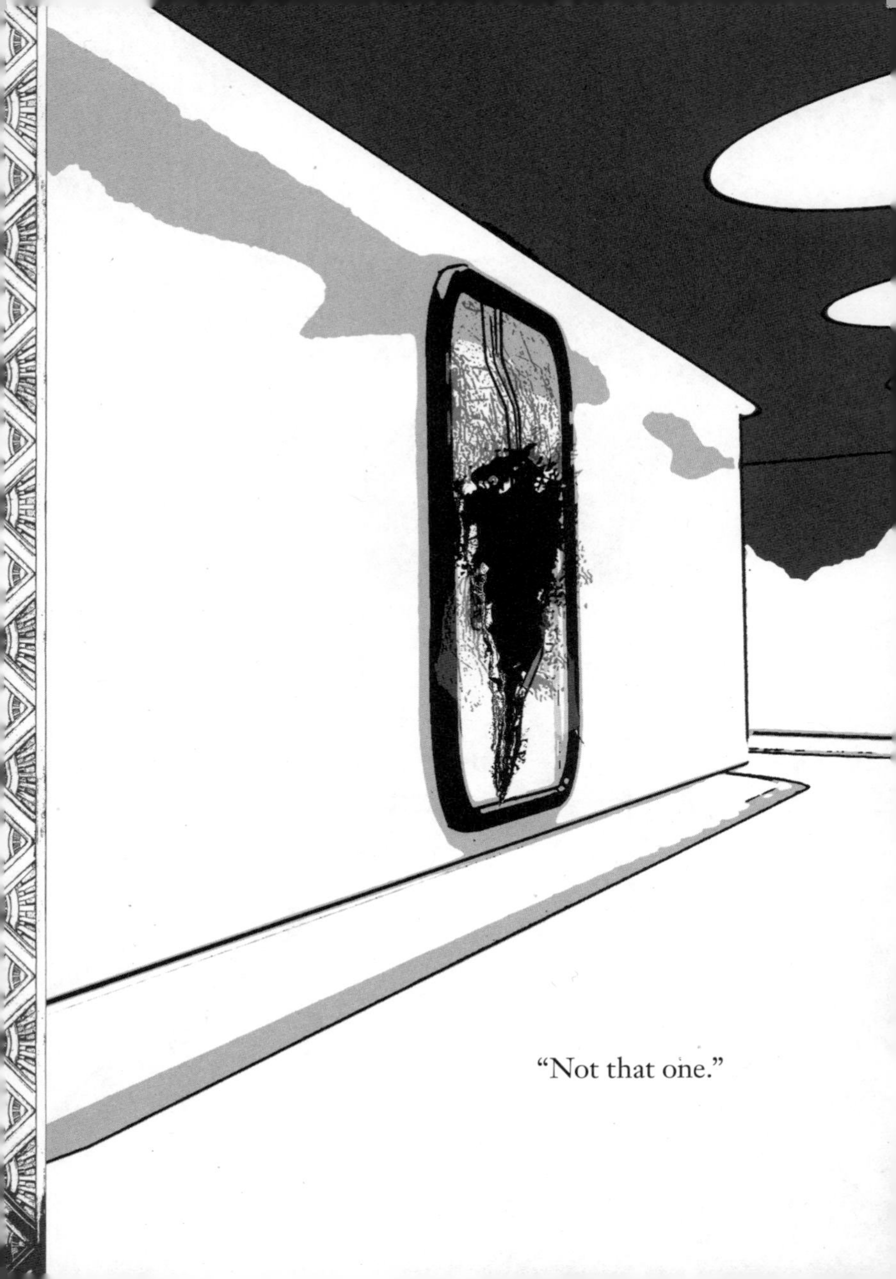
"Not that one."

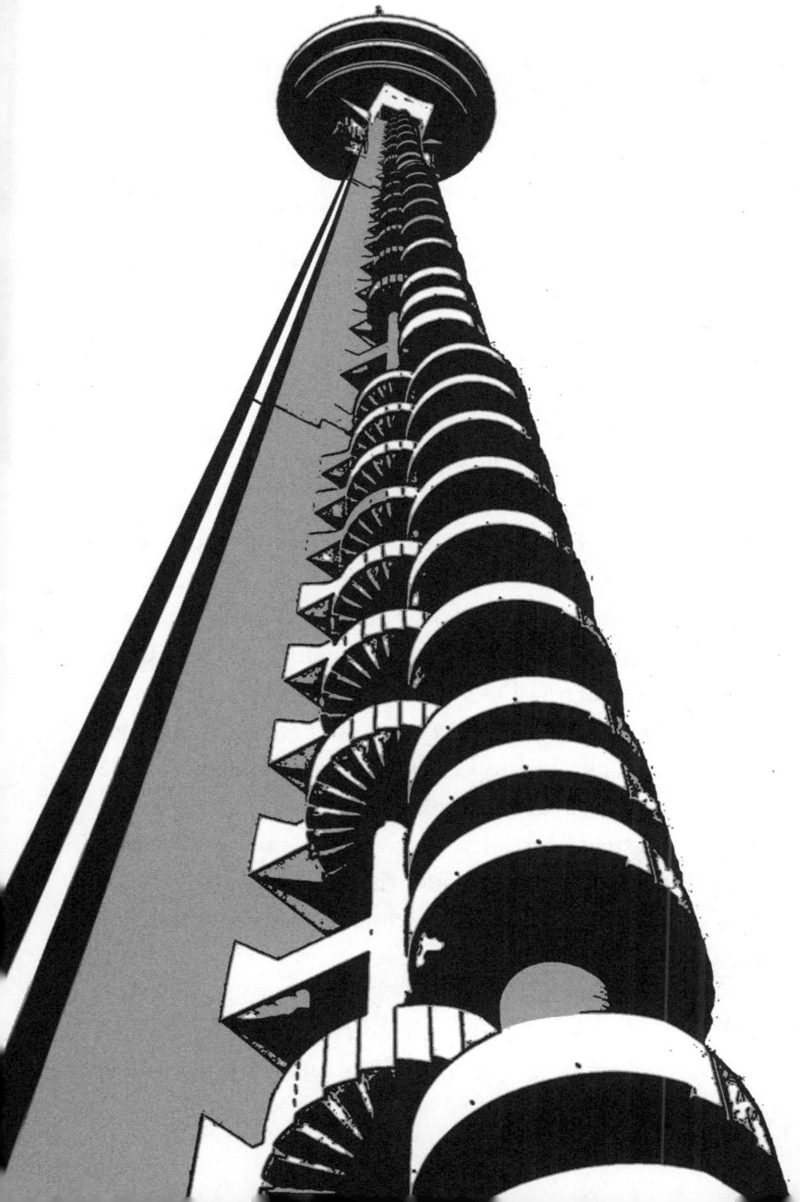

//BLUEBEETLE//

The city centre dwelling stacks with all their interlaced automations were great because you didn't have to sleep in restaurants or supermarkets or laundromats or dry cleaning places. You could slip into a suite and just use what was already on. There was no need to force a lock either, lots of people had left the doors open in the rush to escape.

They took shelter in a condo in Skyhigh Plaza, a beautiful near-modern building with an interior that looked poured from chrome. The condo was an open concept with a clear view of the skyline from every space. The dining room was a fold-up and hung halfway between uses, making the space partially converted to a bedroom. The newspapers were piled up under their delivery printer like a pile of dead fish. A dried out chicken lay shrivelled and unappetizing in a glass dome oven in the central island of the dining area.

In the kitchen, Kerion pushed the revolving shelves without clicking the button, setting the gears grinding.

They were full of canned food. But cans were heavy. Further back, there was a package of dried vitamin wafers. In the corps, he had kept twenty days of meal-pills in his pocket, but they didn't make those anymore, he was sure. Too old-fashioned, and not that good for you. A box of powdered wheatgrass. A carton of heavy plant protein water from the fridge.

"What's it doing, Dad?" Barry asked, pointing at the autorob.

The blue beetle shape of the autorob was moving back and forth over the shadow of a dark stain on the white carpet.

"Cleaning."

Barry went over to the autorob and flipped it upside down with his foot. It beeped an alarm, then turned off in futility.

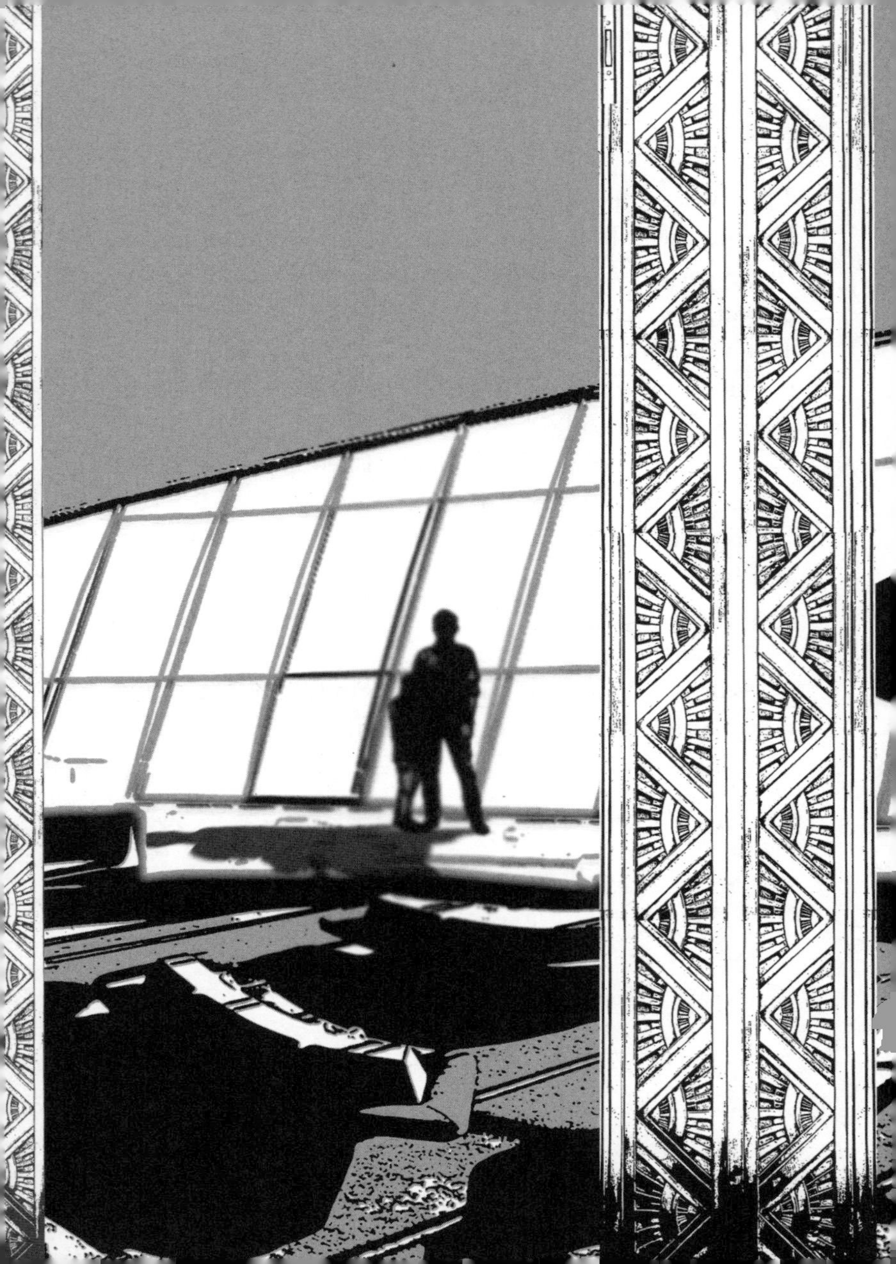

//PARADE//

The city at night was a wonder. Spears of light reaching for the heavens, the dwelling stacks glittering and shimmering in displays of luminous poetry, the parade of automobile headlights, taillights the other, flowing like rivers over causeways and interchanges. And now, the far off firefly lights of the flying platforms as the autovolts systematically swept another city stack. Kerion thought he understood the pattern. They had time to sleep.

"Can I, Dad?" Barry asked as he took the DayDreamer from his backpack. He removed the fairy tale book, too. It had a deep gouge in it from autovolt's knife.

"If you want, sure."

Barry put the DayDreamer on. Kerion used the artificial privacy it created to drop his pretense. He rummaged his pack and took the last three NoPains from the blister pack. He chewed them and washed it down with a fresh squeezed orange juice from the fridge dispenser. Kerion lifted his shirt. The hole was in his abdominal chassis. It was leaking amniotic fluid, the sort that kept infection and tissue rejection at bay. The heat transfer from the phosphor had burnt his skin across the top of the chassis. He found some pliers in the drawer and dug out the bullet tip. He held it up. Turned it. Then he noticed Barry staring at him. He let the shirt fall back and dropped the pliers in the sink.

"I thought you were—" he started.

"The DayDreamer's broken," Barry said. "Does it hurt?"

"No. It didn't go deep, or hit any moving parts. Here, help me plug in." He spooled out the recharge line and passed in to Barry. The boy took it and plugged it in beside the glass dome stovetop.

Kerion motioned to the DayDreamer. "We're both stuck here, I think."

"Hmm?"

"In the real world, I mean."

"As long as we're together, Dad, I'm okay."

A tiny tyrannosaurus ran across the room, followed closely by a silvery spaceman. Then a toy truck with eyes for headlights chased after them. A doll toddled after, then a teddy bear. Perpetuals.

Barry reached his hand toward his father. Kerion took it and they moved after the toys, then stopped.

"I'm still plugged in," Kerion said.

"Just wait until they come by again."

When the parade went past, father and son stomped them into pieces.

//RECYCLEAFTERUSE//

Barry took the folded pages of the comic from where it was hidden in the pages of the old fairy tale book. It was a colour printout on real paper. Paper printing was rare. Not as rare as his mom's old book, but rare. There were only a few places that did it, and you had to bring paper to feed into the slot in exchange for the paper it gave you. He had carefully torn out two pages of the fairy tale book and fed it to the machine to get these two pages of comics. Along the top and bottom edge of the pages was the friendly reminder RECYCLE AFTER USE. He thought about how mad his mom would have been if she had caught him doing that. She would have used that rare invocation of his full name, Batholomew. That's how he'd know the weight of it.

He had been so mad after the divorce. Is that why he had done it? Barry knew his dad would be mad if he found these too. He also knew it was ironic that he hid them inside his mom's old fairy tale book. But he had put them there, in the place of the pages he had traded. The pages were nostalgic, he understood that word now. A reminder of a simple happy time. A memory that was also a little bit of a lie. It felt good to lie to yourself sometimes. He guessed that's what made nostalgia dangerous.

The printed comic pages were from a newsreel that he had loved while his father was away. It showed the Jet Jumper suits of the Unionized Marines, all polish and flash, their leader, his helmet off, winking and assuring Barry that "We're in this fight to win it. Be home before you know it!" In the next panel, he put on his helmet and in the next he joined his comrades in jet assisted leaps across a battlefield. The comic made the Jet Jumpers look invincible. It was how he had thought of his father then, invincible. He told every kid at school about the Unionized Marines, how he was going to join as soon as he could. He was earning school credits to cover his dues. He memorized every publicized statistic about the JJS, confident that he and his dad would talk about nothing else upon his return. How he would impress his father with his confident working knowledge of the JJS. His dad, proud and jovial, would tell him about his adventures in the war. They would laugh and talk about how soon it would be until Barry could get himself in a Jet Jumper. How maybe his dad could bend the rules and get him into a Unionized Marine HQ and show him how it really worked. The folded pages made him feel the elation of that potential future until he returned suddenly to the room he sat in.

There were only things as they were.

Barry's naive expectation had widened into a chasm of disappointment that made his heart hurt, not only for himself, but for his father, who had been fooled by a promised future, and his mother, who he could not bring himself to think of too often.

"She would be proud of you," Kerion said.

Barry said nothing.

"Please know that I, I understand the guilt you feel,"— Kerion couldn't look right at his son—"at surviving."

"It's that, and it's…" Barry was still and quiet, but his hands were shaking.

"You can tell me. You can talk to me, love. I'll listen."

"It's not fair!" Barry blurted, tears bursting. "It's that I know she'd be here too. It would have been the three of us. All of us together, and that all this wouldn't seem so hopeless if she were here too. But she got sick and that isn't fair. It isn't fair that we go on being clever and being brave and being strong against all of this, but she got sick. She was smarter and braver than me. If I'm here, she would be too. Most of *you* is gone and *you're* still here. Some of her was sick and it took all of her! It's not fair!" Barry grabbed the edge of the fairy tale book and flung it away.

He kicked at his coverings, a futile gesture, wanting to strike at something, anything.

"It's normal to feel mad at her."

"I'm mad at you."

"I know. But you need to know. She didn't give up or give in."

"Then what!? Why?"

"Some fights are over when they start."

Barry wept.

"You leaving didn't make her sick," Barry said.

"If I had stayed—her last year would have been different," Kerion said. He was staring into a memory, his eyes wet.

"You leaving didn't make her sick," Barry said.

"When I think about her, I cry," Kerion said. "I miss her. But your Grandpa told me something that helps. To say 'Thank you' instead of 'I miss you' when you think of her."

Kerion didn't say what else he was thinking. That he would trade places with her if he could, or that it made him feel guilty that he enjoyed being the one that was looking after Barry. He lamented the loss of simple uncomplicated love, but also wondered if there had ever been such a thing.

"Why can't the DayDreamer make her come back for me?" Barry asked.

"I don't know. It doesn't work for me either."

Kerion crossed the distance between them, dropped to his knees, and took Barry into his arms. Relishing the warmth of his son's body against the parts of his that still felt such things.

"Maybe because it doesn't understand that the hurt it makes you feel is a good hurt."

"It says in that book, in one of the stories, that you aren't an adult until your parents have died."

"Oh Barry."

"I don't want to grow up."

"I don't want you to have to."

//PIECES//

Pieces of an autovolt radio were spread out on the kitchen island. Kerion had found a few tools in the closet press drawers. He tuned it. A binary warble came through on one channel, then another then another then another. Then he heard something else, clear and full through the static and the din of faint signal.

Barry had just come out of the bathroom. Steam from the shower lingered.

"Barry! Listen!"

"I don't—"

"I was hoping we could use the radios to, I don't know, track back their distress calls to find out if anyone else was out there. Or maybe listen in. But it's binary. It was silly really because—"

The radio squawked. Not binary. A scrap of human voice.

"What did it say, Dad?"

"Shhhhh. Listen."

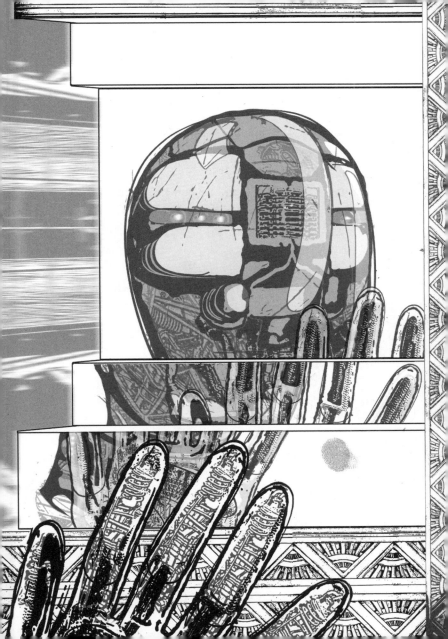

—beck station. If you are receiving this message, head south to Delta City. The resistance is holding at Delta City. This is Lt. Dolby Michaels transmitting from Gernsbeck station. If you are receiving this message—

"What does that mean?"

"It means that your dad knows what train to take."

//ZIPROAR//

They did the dishes themselves, put the food wrappers in the recycle tubes, and pulled the blinds shut. They swept up the broken toys and put them in the electronics recycle tube. Then, Barry flipped over the autorob cleaner. As they pulled the door shut, they heard it chime to life and begin anew to clean the stain on the carpet.

They went to the stairwell and headed for the causeway level.

Barry took the stairs two at a time and rounded the next landing first. Kerion bumped into him at the curve before the next flight of stairs.

Hearthole was waiting in the stairwell landing one floor down. It turned its face and saw them. It started up the stairs. Hearthole's clear shell was blackened on the inside and one leg was shaky. It gripped the guardrail and came for them, dragging up its damaged leg.

"Back, back, get back."

They pushed through the door into the hallway. One side was a transparent wall with a beautiful view of the

Terrance Place. The garden flats, meticulously tended, each a riot of colour and growth. They got to the end of the hall, but there was no stairwell there, only the lift. Kerion thumbed the button. The swoosh of air brought the pneumatic capsule to them. The door whirred open.

"You said not to use the tube."

"I know, I know. Put your foot in the door so it doesn't close. Good, yes, like that."

He knelt and flicked the safety off Newone's rifle, taking aim at the stairwell door at the end of the hall.

Hearthole slammed it open. Startled, Kerion fired and the phosphor round exploded into the wall beside the autovolt. It was coming fast now in a limping jog, knife out. The next shot hit Hearthole in the shoulder, a glance that spun the robot and knocked it down. The third round hit the floor by the robot's head.

Kerion stood up.

"Hold my hand," the boy said. The father did as his son asked, and they stepped backward in the pneumatic elevator. The door shut and they started down a moment before Hearthole slammed against the door.

"Any close ones will be headed here. I pushed the main floor. If it stops anywhere else, I'm going to shoot, okay?"

The boy let go of his hand and grabbed his belt at the back.

"Good boy."

On the 65th floor, the door snapped open and Hearthole's arm piniomed through. His knife edge cut Kerion's cheek deeply. Kerion shot the autovolt in the chest as the door opened all the way. The flash and impact pushed it backward. Barry slapped at the door switch and they were on their way again. Blood pattered on the floor until the main level chime sounded and the door opened.

Something loomed and Kerion fired. A floor mop autorob exploded into bits of chrome and plastic.

"Dad, your face!"

"Come on, love. It's okay. It's okay. Come on."

The zip-roar of the freeway hummed through as hundreds of automobiles shot across twenty lanes. The lift's bottom button had taken them to the automobile claim stack beneath the highrise rather than the pedestrian level. The next car was primed and waiting, the rest were in a lineup, the rail system like soda cans in an automat. The door slid up and the circular lounge of the vehicle, spacious and comfortable, beckoned.

"No, no, no." Kerion turned and tried to reach the tube again, but the door closed.

The railing held them back from the dangers of the cars. No way off but up the next lift or into the waiting car.

The lift chimed as it descended. A shape was visible behind the translucent doors.

"Okay, love, get in the car."

He pushed the boy inside the car and crouched at the door. Hearthole came out of the lift, this close, though Kerion had him centred and right. Click went the rifle, its ammunition already spent. Kerion fell backward and Barry pushed the departure pad and the door swung shut. There was a screech as the tip of the combat knife dug into the enamel of the car door.

Kerion looked at Barry, who looked at him, then the rifle.

"I just…I'm sorry…I just lost count."

"We made it."

Kerion looked around the interior of the vehicle, then out the side window. Beside them only a few metres away and keeping pace, a podcar cruised along, its occupants slumped and quiet against the windows.

"If we can get out."

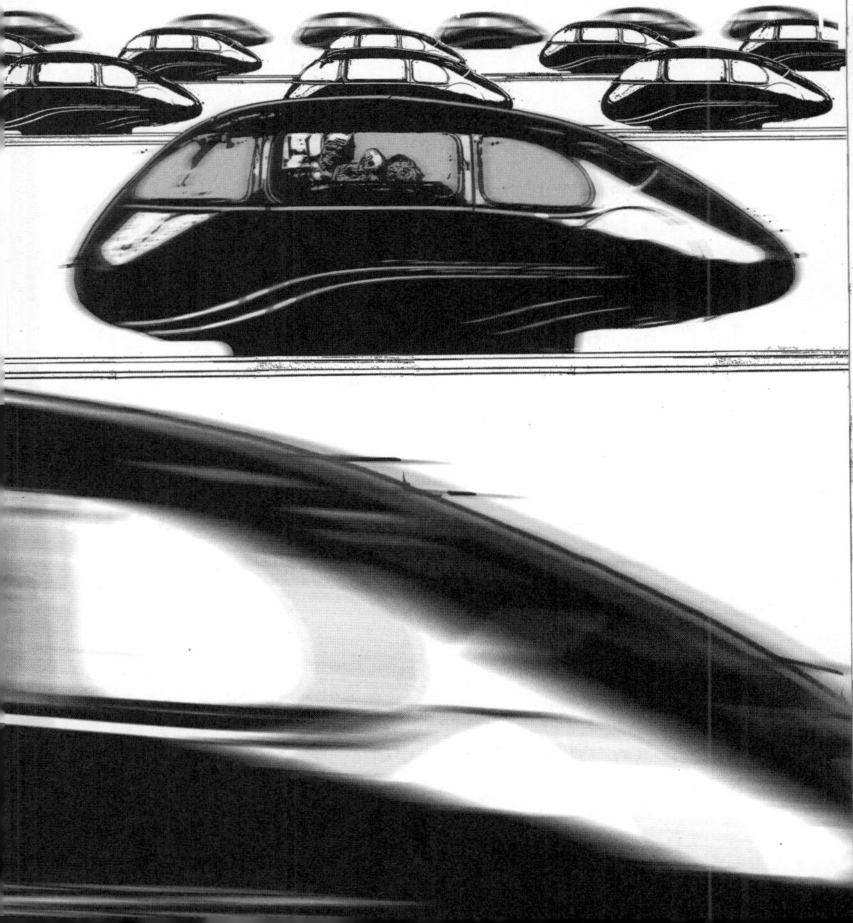

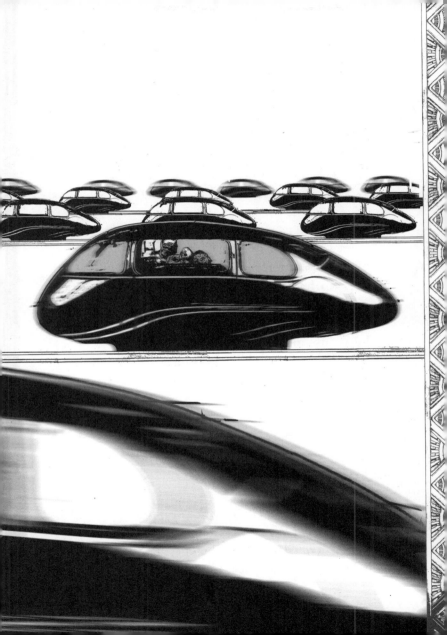

//EVERYTHINGWE'VEGOT//

The freeway.

"Don't look, okay. Just stay down here."

Kerion had looked back and that was a mistake. Hearthole sat prim and proper in the car behind them.

"Please state or enter your desired arrival location," said the automobile.

Fishing for his notebook, Kerion dug out the platform number. They were both lying on the floor of the autocar. He punched in the number.

"Time to destination: twenty-two minutes. Please be aware that the safety lock is enabled."

"He's playing with us, making it last. We're rare now." Kerion said.

"What?"

"Nothing. Here. Have something to eat. Then let's play Everything We've Got."

Barry nodded and started emptying his pockets and then dumped his backpack. Kerion did the same. On the floor was the book of fairy tales with a hundred pages stabbed through. A carton of heavy water. A package of vitamin wafers (four left), seven rolls of automat tokens, a snub-nosed revolver (empty), three VB batteries, four maps, a plastic sandwich box (inside: cheese, half-eaten), two pocket knives, a multi-tool, a bayonet, a autovolt rifle (empty), lots of wrappers, an almost empty tube of SteadyGlue (which they had used to seal Kerion's cheek), the Rocket pistol (two shots) a standard flashlight, a pen flashlight, and one short extension cord still in the package.

"It's bad again," Barry said. "We only do this before it's bad."

"Yes. It's bad. The car won't let us out and—"

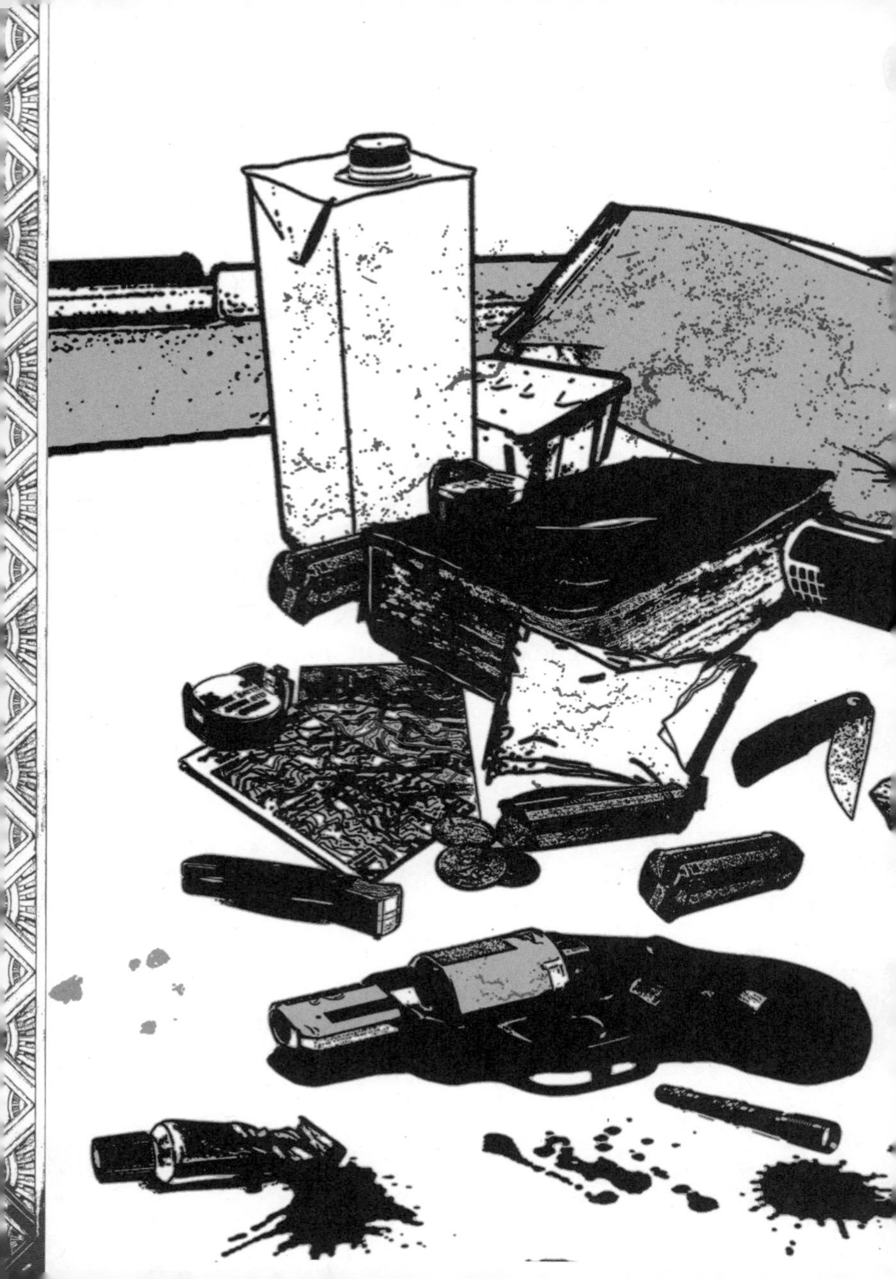

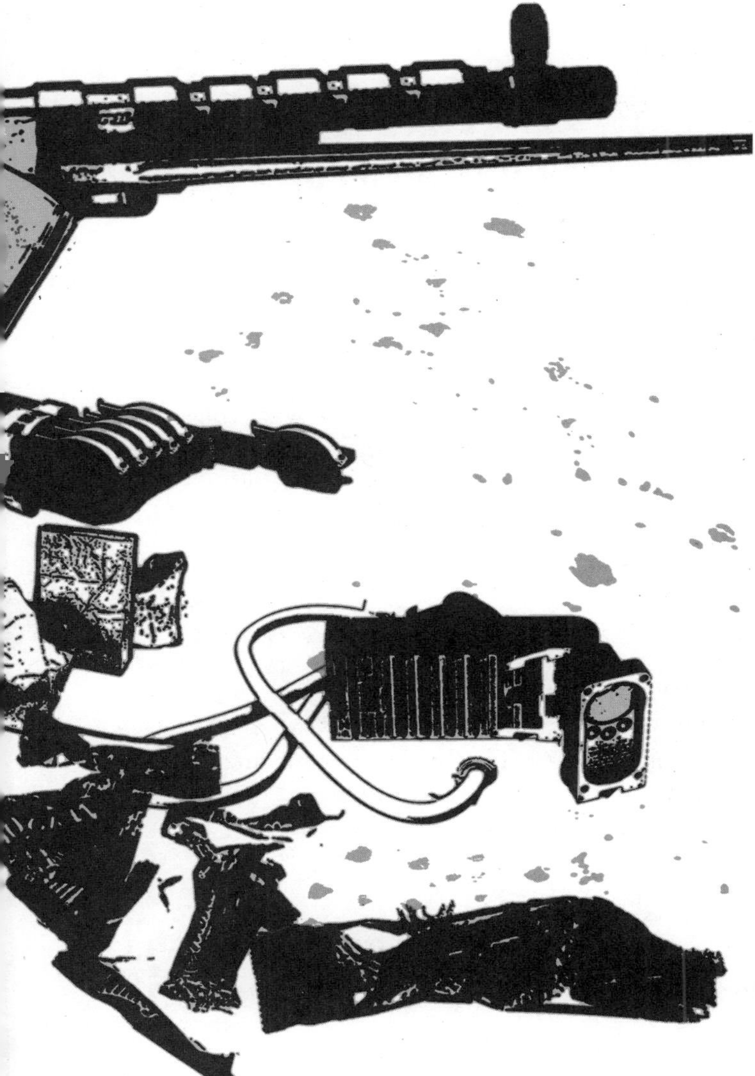

//CANYOUSAYIT//

"Arrival at destination in ten minutes. Be advised that the safety lock is active."

"Disable safety lock." Kerion knew what the automobile would say, but couldn't help himself.

"Unable to comply. Safety lock is active."

He set to work with the multi-tool.

"I told you not to look."

"I know."

"Well?"

"It's right behind us."

"I know."

"It's following us. That's what you meant. It's toying with us."

"I'm sorry."

"I won't leave you."

"What?"

"If you try and fight him. I won't run. I don't care what you say. I'm staying with you."

"Okay."

"Dad?

"Yeah?"

"Can you say it?"

"I love you."

"Can you say it agai—"

"I love you."

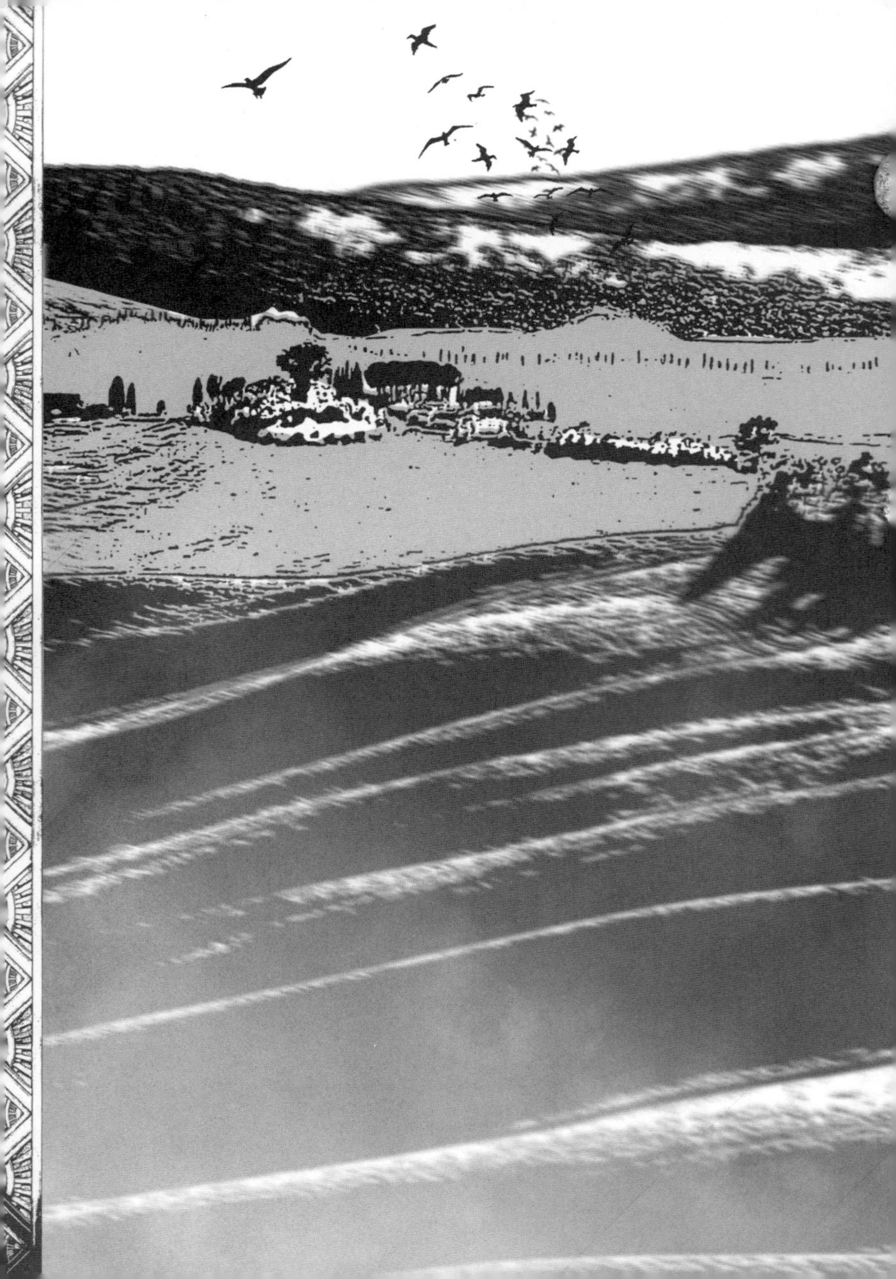

//JUMP//

"Destination will be reached in five minutes. Be advised that the safety lock is active."

"Are you ready?"

He had stripped off all the panels and parts he could with the multi-tool. Kerion had uncovered a foam canister but couldn't figure out a way to use it to help them, and a battery case the size and shape of a milk carton on its side. They had used the knives to strip away all the cushions they could and piled them, and the panel, overtop of Barry for protection.

The glass wasn't going to break from anything they hit it with. He knew from the evidence of the occupied cars around them. If anything dangerous hit the car from the outside, the pod would instantly fill with shock absorbing collision-foam. But the rocket bullet from the astrojumper's gun could shatter it he was sure, though maybe it would ricochet back inside. If it blew up, maybe the pillows would help with the blowback. Even with the window gone, they couldn't jump out of a car at speed and survive. They had to slow it down first. The only thing they had that could crack the battery was the other rocket bullet. One for each job. Only one for each.

Safety protocol in a damaged car would move them off the highway, unclogging the highway artery quickly and efficiently and automatically. There might be access along the safety lane to the pedestrian level. If they got off at the platform, Hearthole would be right behind. They would need to get clear on foot and, well, it was a chance.

The sound of the gun inside the automobile hurt them both. The bullet hurt the car, blowing a fist-sized hole through the mechanisms and revealing the rushing tarmac below. If the car said anything to them, both their ears were ringing too badly to tell. A sudden deceleration occurred, and the car moved not toward the safety lane but across forty lanes of traffic to the far left side of the highway.

"They changed it." Barry said.

Their pod clicked across the lanes, pausing in a rhythm that allowed them to pass between the traffic that shot past.

"No. Nonononono," Kerion said, but couldn't hear himself. "Wrong side, wrong side."

"Dad!"

Kerion looked to Barry

"Dad they changed it. Turned the freeway into a river too fast for anyone that got their car to stop to cross."

Following them through the impenetrable flow of traffic was Hearthole, seated with perfect posture inside of the pursuing autopod.

"You're doing great. But we still have to run." Barry said.

The second shot burst the window and the buzz whine of the traffic flooded in. Kerion got out first, then pulled the boy through. Even as he did it, Kerion knew he had made another critical mistake. If they had waited in the pod, that one shot might have freed them and destroyed the autovolt. He had wasted it on a window. The following car clicked into place.

They were stopped against the rail of the freeway overpass. Over the rail was a drop of twenty stories to an idyllic parkland where he could see birds flocking. The rail lane stretched kilometres in both directions before the first strut. They could run for it, they could try to run across forty lanes of speeding coffin cars that flowed across the freeway, or—

Jump. He'd hold Barry close, hug him tightly and go over the rail, to the end.

"Dad?"

"Some fights are over when they start."

He knelt and took Barry by the shoulders. He looked him right in the eyes. He was aware of the autovolt stepping from the autopod beyond.

"I loved your mother and you very much. I wish I had been there."

"You can't make me run." Barry said, "I won't leave."

Kerion took a big breath.

"We might have to pay for it."

Hearthole limped toward them.

"I think we earned it already, Dad."

Kerion took Barry into his arms. Turbulent air from the speeding automobiles tousled their hair. He pushed his son's hair from his face, kissed him on the forehead, put his arms around him, lifted him in a tight embrace. Held him as he had when he was a toddler. Kerion moved to the rail. He turned.

"Look at that park, that's the part worth keeping."

Hearthole's limb was an audible clink.

"Beautiful."

"Now close your eyes love."

"Okay."

Kerion ran forward into traffic.

//GOSTOPGO//

The first lane was easy because it was a dare. But the shock
of sudden survival made the ordeal of choice a heartbeat
of life and near death. Between each commuter path was
a midlane not quite a meter wide. The automobiles shot
past like bullets and the suction nearly made Kerion fall
over. He looked left, hesitated, and a car shot past. He
went forward one chance at a time. Ten lanes in, two cars
passed him and the boy at the same moment. The combined drag of both pulled him over. He fell hard on both
knees, twisting to keep the boy from hitting the macadam.
He rolled over onto his back as another shot past.

He saw Hearthole. The robot was making a careful
advance, timing each few steps, even with the limp, to
perfectly move between the cars. Kerion forced himself
up, forced himself to ignore the ache of both arms. Ignore
the sobbing of his boy. Ignore everything but what was
in front of him. Go. Stop. Go. Go. Stop. Falter. No. Go.
Go. Go. Stop.

//ALMOST//

They almost made it. Maybe it was the exhilaration that made Kerion careless. Two lanes from the far side, he misjudged by a half second. He didn't feel the impact as the automobile struck him in the foot but registered the sound. The impact flung his leg out behind him, spinning him and throwing both of them to the ground in the final lane. Barry crawled towards him instead of to safety, and it was all Kerion could do to seize his son and roll.

Then they were clear of the freeway. Looking behind them, they saw Hearthole three lanes back, then two. The smoky chassis and the limp made him into a broken windup toy. Kerion saw his own foot bent the wrong way.

"I won't run," Barry screamed.

"Then I won't, either."

Kerion managed to get to his feet just as Hearthole was across the curb, knife leading. Kerion hit Hearthole hard with his shoulder as the automaton reached them, forcing them both back a few steps. The knife slashed at his thigh and would have killed him then, opening the femoral artery, if he were flesh there. The second strike skittered up his abdomen and half of the attack cut deeply across his chest.

An autocar hit Hearthole at tremendous speed. He was just suddenly not there.

Kerion hobbled away toward the off ramp while the sound of sirens told the dead inhabitants of a thousand automobiles that an accident had happened and emergency-robs were en route.

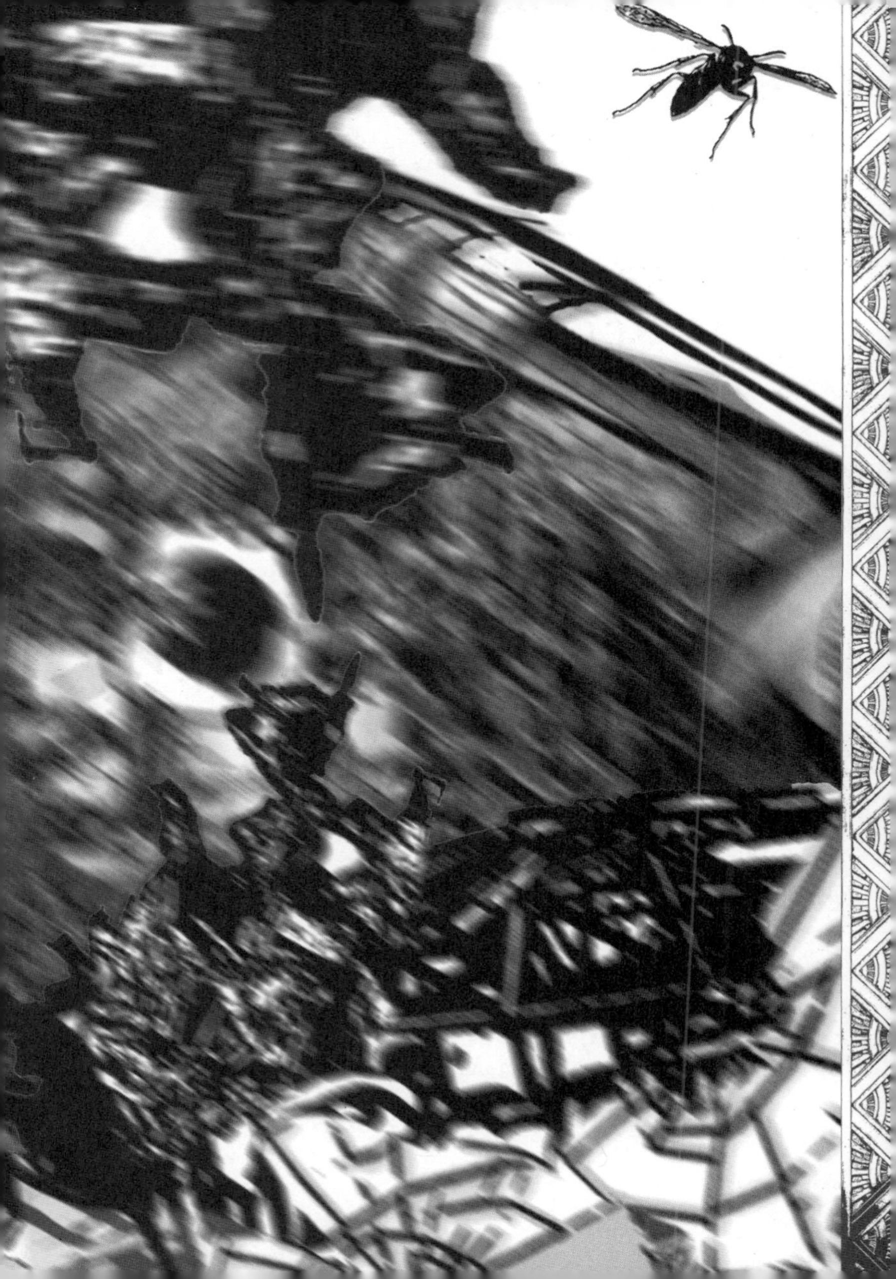

//COMFORTANDCARE//

The platform was empty for them. The supersonic train glided into the station on a feather of magnetism, and the automatic door opened. They each slotted their ticket, purchased from the automatic kiosk, and sat down in first class. Barry had the station's first aid pod in his arms and clicked it open looking for the hand-held medrob. Kerion had a balled up souvenir T-shirt he had taken without paying for pressed to his chest wound. The slogan on the shirt had said: COMFORT and CARE await you in DELTA CITY.

Barry looked down at their ticket display in the mahogany arm rest.

"I thought we were headed south."

"No, son. Everyone who heard that message is headed south. Including the autovolts I'm sure. We're going North. As far as we can. Maybe to a place where the future never happened."

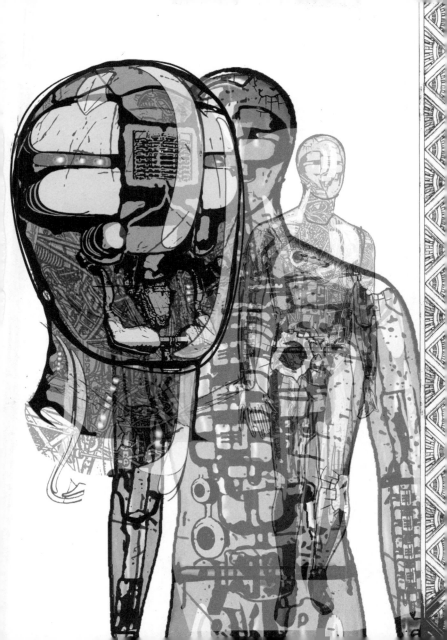